HOUSE, BODY, BIRD

Bernie Jean Schiebeling

ISBN-13: 979-8-89116-021-7

Published by Psychopomp
psychopomp.com

Publisher's Note:
No part of this publication may be reproduced, distributed, or transmitted in any form or by any means, including photocopying, recording, or other electronic or mechanical methods, without the prior written permission of the publisher, except in the case of brief quotations embodied in critical reviews and certain other noncommercial uses permitted by copyright law.

This book is a work of fiction. Names, characters, places, and incidents either are products of the author's imagination or are used fictitiously. Any resemblance to actual persons, living or dead, events, or locales is entirely coincidental.

Cataloging-in-Publication Data
Names: Schiebeling, Bernie Jean, author.
Title: House, Body, Bird
Description: Woodbury, VT : Psychopomp [2026]
Identifiers: ISBN: 9798891160217 (paperback)
Subjects: LCSH: Horror fiction. |
BISAC: FICTION / Horror. |

Cover & interior formatted by Christine M. Scott
clevercrow.com

Cover illustration by John G. Reinhart

FOR MY PARENTS, WHO ENCOURAGED ME
TO GET OUT OF THE HOUSE,
AND WHO ALWAYS WELCOMED ME BACK IN.

TABLE OF CONTENTS

HOUSE 5

BODY 61

BIRD 141

PROLOGUE

MY FATHER presses the key into my mother's forehead, and she swings open.

A split down the middle. A hairline crack in her lip-sticked smile. Blue eyes once locked on me, now staring glassy into opposite corners of the basement.

I stumble back, falling, cold stones against my palms. Her throat, her stomach. Carving apart, neat and bloodless, rib cage splaying. From inside, an amber glow glitters off the clinking charm bracelets on her thin, languid wrists, shines on my gaunt father's glasses as he moves to block the stairs. My mother *opens* like a dollhouse welcoming a child.

I scream. Scramble to the wall. Jostle the creaking shelves, knock free the archival boxes. They scatter around me, spill all the tiny people not needed for the museum-worthy houses upstairs. Mother dolls in long skirts and placid smiles. Daughter dolls in pigtails and rosy cheeks. White dogs and ginger cats. Cloth and paper, wood and plastic. Ceramic, shattering. A broken blue eye meeting mine.

My mother. No face, no body left to recognize now, just the spaces inside, divided in that familiar way. Bedroom in her right breast, bathroom and closet in the left. Kitchen below, and dining, and parlor. All perfectly furnished: the little bed with its patchwork coverlet, woven rugs on the hardwood floor, the ruby sparkle of something wet and living beneath. Shifting with a steady pulse behind the floral wallpaper. Trembling red above the gold-wire chandelier and matchstick furniture. Spotless tiles giving way to copper plumbing entwined with her veins, ceiling molding tracing her clavicle, a spiral staircase winding up her throat, past her lolling tongue, into the attic of her skull.

A perfect miniature of my mother stands there, looking out at me. As though she's just far away. As though I'm seeing her atop a distant hill. The scattered dolls waver in my vision: grasping hands, open mouths, a thousand sightless eyes. I don't understand.

Lila, I've never understood.

HOUSE

"YOU DON'T HAVE TO GO," Lila said, folding a shirt her girlfriend had thrown into the open suitcase. She placed the tidy black square atop the others. Birdie had asked her not to do retail shit on her day off, but Birdie wasn't looking. "You know that, right?"

Birdie responded with two more T-shirts flung over her narrow shoulders, then with, "I'm not going because I *have* to. I'm going 'cause I *want* to."

Just five days in the museum her parents passed off as a home—with dollhouses stacked ceiling-high in every room and tourists nosing around like her family's life was an exhibit—but it paid to pack for more. Last time, the kitchen sink had started leaking the day before she was due to leave. And then there were the mice going after the Victorian room, chewing all that delicate wooden trim like its namesake gingerbread. And she'd needed to help her mother put up flyers for another lost neighborhood dog, though at least that had gotten her out of the window-and-door-clotted house. Birdie had spent a couple hours in town, breathing grassy air and stapling *Lost Dog* above other *Missing* and *Have You Seen Me?* flyers fading on telephone poles. Looking at all those animal eyes photocopied into oblivion, she'd gotten a prickle up her spine and finally left.

But that was five years ago, when Birdie was twenty-two and stupid. Her parents had shrunk with age. On the museum website, she'd seen photos of them standing alongside their biggest miniature, a huge Georgian manor that opened to reveal a dozen smaller Georgian manors stashed inside. Her stooped parents could practically live in that dollhouse now. Birdie couldn't look away from her mother's eyes, which shone the way they did only when she'd been crying and trying to hide it.

They just needed help with renovations. Her mom had whispered her father's weakness into the phone like she was afraid talking about it would break his hip. "And," her mom had said, "there won't be any guests." No strangers murmuring right outside her bedroom while Birdie tried to sleep in.

Birdie leaned against the closet's folding doors, but tension ran through every line in her tall, pale body. Ceramic with a cracked glaze. She wound her brittle bleached curls around her fingers and saw that Lila wouldn't dignify her lie of "wanting to" with the bare minimum of pitying belief. Her girlfriend's eyes were slits, turning all their gold-brown glitter into dark accusation. Birdie's low-ceilinged studio apartment provided no hiding places.

"You've bitten your fingernails bloody, Bird," Lila said. Birdie hid her hand behind her back like an oversized kid. "Your bathroom trash is, like, half fingernails."

"That's where fingernails go."

"Right, but—" Lila folded up her knee-socked legs on Birdie's neatly made bed, rumpling the patchwork quilt. "What if I came with you? Make the visit go more quickly, create distractions for quick getaways."

Birdie's pointy face twitched. "No. They're not—" She remembered her mother's averted gaze, her father's rage-red throat. She turned back to the closet. "I'm not bringing you around my shitty family."

Lila sighed. "Remember our fourth date? The potluck?"

Of course Birdie remembered. She'd always thought of it as their first *real* date, since Lila had specifically asked Birdie to be her plus-one. Before that, Lila had just handed Birdie her flyers, hand-lettered and sticker-rich, copied and printed on pastel paper. Always for parties at the town's only gay bar. Lila always just saying, "You should come." And Birdie always went, if only to pass ice waters to Lila between strawberry margaritas.

So Lila had seen those parties as dates too? A little warmth kindled in Birdie's rib cage, but she snuffed it out. *Focus.*

The bedsprings creaked as Lila bounced up and wrapped her arms around Birdie's waist from behind. "At the potluck, I got you some chips and ranch and salsa and guac, because *way* too many people decided to bring chips and dips, and then you saved the day—"

"It was just coupons." The benefits of being a delivery driver who didn't get out much. Lila's voice purring between her shoulder blades made it hard to think, and Birdie pulled away to keep sorting through the clothes. Regret twinged in her stomach as Lila's flower-tattooed wrists slipped free.

"Sure, B. But before you *saved the day*, I told you that my family was huge. Like, 'taking up a whole subway car just with first cousins' type of huge. Whatever your parents said, good or bad, I've heard it twice from my aunties and uncles. I can handle it."

"I don't need you to handle it." She'd never told Lila about her folks. It'd made things easier. Everything in its proper place. Lila hadn't pressed her about it, not then or any other time during the eight months they'd been together.

Ten months, actually, since Lila counted those parties. Birdie needed to get her shit together. Figure out a good anniversary gift. Lila probably already had something picked out, some weird and impractical and perfect thing she'd found rummaging through tag sales. Something like the candle-topped coyote skull or foot-shaped teapot that had both surprised Birdie with how well they fit into her tiny apartment. Her tiny life.

Of course, when Lila had asked if she could have a dresser drawer at Birdie's place, Birdie had still seized up, joked dry-mouthed about Lila needing a new place to put all the bobby pins tucked into her black curls. She'd stumbled over her "Maybe, I don't know" response when Lila showed her cheap apartments over Main Street storefronts. She'd even blurted, "I don't like dogs," when Lila had cooed over the rescue pitties at a local adoptathon. That night, her forehead on her steering wheel, she'd apologized to Lila over the phone. "I don't know why I said that. I get along fine with the dogs I meet on deliveries."

"Duh." Lila had sniffled a little. "My roommate gets allergies when you come over. You're so full of dander."

"Mostly just full of shit, though."

"Ha." It wasn't really a laugh. "Just...let me in some-time, you know?"

That had been almost three months ago. Lila kept close to Birdie like a friend knocking at a front door, and Birdie kept her hand on the doorknob, not quite ready to answer.

Now, Lila ducked in front of Birdie. She reached up, played with the hair on the nape of Birdie's neck. Birdie managed not to flinch as Lila's warm fingers skated over a gnarled scar.

"What if—" She raised her thick brows, eyes sparkling. "I said I'm married to some finance bro?"

Birdie snorted. Like that would work. Not with the shakily scripted *dyke!* in stick-and-poke black on her large, soft bicep. Not with Lila's ongoing love affair with tank tops, which Birdie usually endorsed wholeheartedly. "Please be serious."

"I am serious! You're treating this like a death sentence—"

"I'm not. This is a normal trip."

"Yes, you're being very normal. I'm just saying, we could have *fun* together."

Birdie stared at Lila. She probably thought of this as a countryside outing, clean meadow and mountain air, roadside maple syrup stands. Playing house together in a place with real wood furniture on real wood floors, far away from their separate thin-walled apartments. A chance to see their toothbrushes together in the same glass.

How long could that idea survive, once her parents stuck Lila in the black-and-white bedroom, and she had to wake up under the dusty smiles of all the hetero wedding dioramas?

For the second time, Birdie gently unhooked herself from Lila's embrace. "Babe. I'm packing."

Lila huffed, collapsed back onto the bed. "And I'm helping. I guess."

"It's your day off. You can stop—"

"Look. I'm not sure why you're going back, but if you have to visit the world's creepiest dollhouse, I don't want you to be there alone. I'm your *partner*, Birdie."

"Li, we don't even live together."

Behind her, Lila let out a tiny breath, the littlest gut punch. Birdie froze, her eyes locked on a strappy gold dress. Lila had left it here after New Year's, one of the only pieces of herself permanently in Birdie's home.

Birdie should have known it wasn't about a fun outing. She should look at her girlfriend. She should say something.

Babe, you're too sensitive.

Or: *Lila, I'm sorry.*

Or: *We don't live together. What, you want me to lie about it?*

Or: *I'll think about it. I promise.*

She should be better at this by now. Birdie dragged the dress off its hanger with jerky marionette movements and tossed her next words over her shoulder. "Take you out for dinner before I go?"

Her nonchalance flopped. Lila sighed. "Promise me you'll call if things get weird."

"We could get that pizza you like." Why was her mouth moving? Sometimes, Birdie saw Lila smile when she spotted the gold dress. She hung it back up.

Five days in her childhood bedroom, suburbia looming over her. Shelves lined with white picket fences and neat square houses with primary-colored doors. Mother dolls gardening, daughter dolls chasing the dog, their feet glued to the lawn (she'd learned that early when she'd wanted to play with them). At night, glowing windows silhouetted the father dolls inside.

"Birdie." Lila's quiet voice was like a plea through a keyhole.

Birdie could have crossed the room to her girlfriend, kissed her lotioned knuckles and her roller-skating-scarred knees. She could have left the wrinkles in the quilt once they stood up to go to dinner. She could have unpacked her suitcase and asked Lila to stay.

Instead, she packed the neatly folded clothes without comment. She threw her luggage in the back seat. At dinner, she mostly stared at the pizza between them. When she dropped Lila off afterwards, Birdie seized her hand. Lila turned, hopeful, the amber streetlights catching half her round face and haloing her black curls.

Birdie could have said she would call.

"I'll be home soon," Birdie said.

Soon. She'll be home soon. The House is calling her as it has called the Family for generations. The House knows her homecoming like aching bones know the arrival of rain, and the House remembers her as a scar memorializes the pain of a wound.

Hands clutching doorknobs. Legs dangling from windows. Footsteps hesitating halfway up the stairs. Fragile heartbeats passing through fingertips into wallpaper, faint whispers bouncing back from ceilings. Holding her breath, back against the wall under the bed, elbows drawn close in the attic's corner shadows, meat motionless among the dinner table's forks and knives. Waiting for the heavy step. Waiting for the growling and the grip. The years of fury rumbling through the walls.

She'll walk the halls she walked before, place footprint into footprint. Sleep in the ghost-grave of her childhood bed, dig for spoons in the same drawers. She'll remember as the House does, and the House remembers long after hands have stilled and bones have crumbled and souls have dissipated. The House remembers, and it calls the Daughter home.

————

The unpaved drive to the museum seemed longer with every visit, gravel crunching endlessly as Birdie rolled through the deep forest. Low maples hung over her car, branches scraping the roof. If it weren't for the tourist dollars the museum brought the postfactory, posteverything town a couple miles away, no one would ever wander into this part of New England. Hell, if it weren't for the signs that her parents put up—sturdy, cheap dollhouses next to plywood arrows with faded paint, urging drivers *Onwards! to the Goodbain Miniatures Museum*—people probably still would have turned around.

A light drizzle dripped off the dollhouses' roofs and the chipped-away faces of the tiny families waving outside them. As a kid, Birdie had liked these houses best, even if teenagers from town took potshots at the windows and chipmunks chewed off the dolls' outstretched arms. If she could've lived in one of those homes, Birdie would've stared out at the vast wilderness with wonder. A pioneer of a quarter acre, a hermit content with her small solitude. She tightened her grip on the steering wheel as her salt-rusted sedan bumped over potholes into the unmowed meadow, and the museum itself emerged against the gray sky.

At first glance, it was a typical Victorian, if a bit confused between Romanesque and Stick styles. The obligatory turret hunching off to one side, the high bay windows glinting like a haughty stare, the suggestion of a mazelike interior and a hand-waving mélange of floors. But the entryway itched in the corner of Birdie's eye, as it always did, and she found her gaze tracing the simple rectangular facade of the old Federal farmhouse. A wide porch and all the other additions had nearly buried its stark, symmetrical windows, but Birdie could find them. Her father had made sure of it, his grip on her child-head pointing her like a dog seized by the scent of prey. "We build on what came before us," he told her, breath hot against her ear. "When a home no longer holds us, we build, and build, and build."

Sometimes Birdie dreamed about running for the front door, open at the end of the long hall. The moon-silvered meadow and spangled black sky stretched wide beyond the dim porch. But as she sprinted, the halls contracted until she was forced to crawl. She always woke before she crossed the threshold. On the nights when Lila slept over, Birdie rolled into her side, and that was a kind of escape.

Birdie's chest hurt, but just a little. She threw the car into park at the bottom of the walnut tree, in case she needed to climb out her bedroom window and make a run for it—which of course she wouldn't need to do. A joyful cry came muffled into the car. Birdie fixed a smile on her face just in time for her mom to fling open the door and tug Birdie's wrists. The stale, coffee-tinted air of a long drive spent wishing for sleep and a good reason to stop rushed out, replaced with the smell of rain and her mom's perfume.

"Oh, Bridget! Ooh, welcome home." She hugged Birdie tight. The crown of her silver head just brushed Birdie's collarbone, and the daughter found herself holding her mother as though she were made of twigs and paper. When the older woman pulled back, Birdie saw that her blue eyes were bright and sunken. A Band-Aid stretched across the middle of her veined hairline. Birdie reached for it.

"Mom, are you—"

Her mom snatched Birdie's hand from the air, her grip tight. For a second, her gaze darted towards the house. Birdie froze—so her father was back there.

"I'm clumsy, is what I am," her mother said, laughing. "Come inside. You must be hungry, and your father's been waiting for lunch."

She headed for the door, her fingers clenched a bit too hard around Birdie's wrist, and Birdie let herself be drawn into the house.

———

If the House were its own creation, one could say that it bided its time over the centuries, nibbling the years off generation upon generation of its loyal family. But outside hands were the only ones who built the House, and the House was only ever a monstrous body, a gasping cadaver walled in by its own ribs. The Goodbain ancestors—expelled from some long-vanished town for now-forgotten crimes—began with a wayward colonial cottage and a damp, mossy cellar hole. The Father sometimes says the crimes were witchcraft. The Father says their Son carried on their legacy. He tells a good story.

The House knows that there was a Daughter too. Her bones were restful, even as moldy thatch transformed to respectable brick and slate shingles. Even as gables rose like crooked limbs over the dusky woods, and high windows blinked into the golden sunrise, the Daughter showed her teeth in the dark. Smiling.

There is always a Daughter in bad times, isn't there? The Grandfather of the Father of the Father of the Father decided to fill the House with houses like a lover filling with memories of his beloved. He did this for a Daughter—the best Daughter of the Victorian age. If he could catch her in her labyrinthine girlhood, he thought, then maybe—

But the House does not know what he thought. A living house is a living body, a disobedient child, a wayward beast. A house is a body is a horror.

The House only remembers.

Floor-to-ceiling shelves of stained walnut wood went up on the walls, and then the split-open handmade houses with their matchbox tables and thread-spool chairs and clothes peg people. They pinched the hallways narrow as castle passages. Old-fashioned electric fixtures sprouted from the walls like steadying wrought-iron hands, their spiral-filamented bulbs casting long shadows across the houses and their occupants in an endless amber twilight.

Newer, painstakingly crafted exhibits—sometimes bought off private collectors, more often made in the basement workspace—sprawled into the parlor, the drawing room, the unused bedrooms upstairs. Countryside manors and town Victorians hung over imitation Chippendale couches and dust-covered trundle beds. Elaborately stacked single-room dioramas crowded on the knobble-legged Queen Anne sideboard and formal twelve-person dining table. Skinny row houses and tenements filled china cabinets and bookshelves like interwoven fingers.

From there, it was a short leap to the attic, the drawing room, the closets, the kitchen, the everywhere-else. The museum-house drew in around itself like one long held breath, ready to recount an inheritance of little homes, a cautionary tale for anyone with elbows. The newest Daughter was mostly elbows. By the time she was born, only a few closets and the basement remained untouched.

But the newest Daughter didn't go into the basement anymore.

———

Birdie's father ate his lunch in the basement studio and remained there through dinner, but Birdie still nearly dropped her mug when someone shuffled up behind her the next morning. A few drops of hot coffee scattered on the floor and singed Birdie's fingertips.

"Careful, sweetie." Birdie's mom smiled at her and reached for the coffeepot. "Good morning."

She should've known it wasn't him. She hadn't had time to do anything wrong yet. Once, at around eleven years old, a cup she'd forgotten to wash had whistled past her ear and broken against the wallpaper. The dent it left disturbed the neat indigo lines and their twining roses. Birdie's father picked at parenthood like fingernails at a scab, seeking restoration of the bodily temple through the excision of its grosser parts. Unless she was fucking up, she barely saw him.

"Morning. Sorry." Birdie grabbed the paper towels from behind a spice rack showcasing dollhouse cutlery. When she knelt to clean the spill, she was shorter than her mom for the first time since early adolescence.

"Did you talk to your father yesterday?" Her mother poured coffee into one of the three mugs they could fit into the cabinets alongside the historical kitchen miniatures. She set a tipped-over butter churn the size of her pinky upright. Birdie hadn't noticed that she'd knocked it over.

"Yeah."

She'd called *hello* down the basement stairs, her heart hammering, her nostrils full of the damp, bitter smell. She'd expected to see her dad waiting down there, staring up through the huge glasses he'd worn since the eighties, his jaw set and trembling. But it was just cold, clean, empty rock. The aged stones, worn and gray as ground-down molars, shone dull under the solitary corded lightbulb. Birdie hated that light, its taunting place near the bottom of the pitch-dark stairs, its pull-cord switch always out of reach until it fluttered against her face like a moth. She always felt like she'd slip, crash into all the dusty houses not fit for display. They slumped into view at the edges of the pooling light, junk her father kept saying he'd fix, spilling from shelves and archival boxes into random stacks and garbage bags. It decayed faster than he could repair it. Always had.

When she was very young—before she knew better—she descended the basement stairs every day to seek him out, to play with the dollies that no one wanted upstairs, to lay her curly head against his thin bicep as he worked, to feel him freeze. Why did he go so still? She never knew, just enjoyed looking at whatever house he was working on and imagining the itsy-bitsy ladies in dresses admiring the two giants who gave them life. She breathed in the serene tomb-scent of the basement, reveled in the sharp paint and peppermint smells that rose from her father's crisp shirtsleeves.

"But did you go catch up with him?" Her mother's sparse silver eyebrows were perfect concerned arches.

"I don't like the basement."

"Surely you don't dislike the basement more than you love your father?" Her mother blew steam off her coffee, her blue eyes gentle and hopeful, except for when they flicked to the basement door.

Christ, Birdie thought. What, was he sleeping down there too? And then she felt stupid, like a kid who thinks their kindergarten teacher curls up beneath the desks. She crumpled the paper towel. "I'm gonna go for a walk."

Her mother sighed. "Of course, sweetie. But make sure you change into something appropriate before the guests get here." She nodded at Birdie's oversized black T-shirt, which depicted a wriggling cadre of bloody skulls.

Birdie stopped in the middle of pulling her sneakers onto bare feet. "You said you were closing. No tourists." She straightened, nearly bashing her shoulder into a scale model of Thomas Jefferson's kitchen. "That's the whole reason I came? To help you with renovations?"

Her mother tapped her fingernails against her mug. "We rescheduled. Your father's projects…" An apologetic smile ghosted over her lips, asking Birdie to understand.

Birdie did not understand. She stormed out through the cruddy gift shop, conveniently located in the mudroom, laid her shoulder into the stuck-in-the-frame door, and hit the ground running. Her mother's last words vanished.

Plume-tipped meadow grass whipped against her bare calves, and she sprinted until the need to monitor her breathing outweighed her stomach-rotting guilt at ignoring her mother, her heartaching rage at her father and his garbage houses, her resigned half-plans for what shirt she'd wear once the tourists arrived.

When she reached the meadow's edge, Birdie flopped onto her back, the muscles in her legs twinging pleasantly. Grass waved above her face, framing a rain-washed blue sky. Clean summer air filled her lungs with the scent of sunshine and dirt and all the weird creatures living in it. Her phone buzzed in her pocket.

A message from Lila: *Thinking of you <3.* Birdie snorted. Lila texted like an abandoned aunt when she was worried. She sat up, brushing leafy bits out of her hair as another message arrived: *You okay so far?*

Birdie started typing *no. parents are* and then deleted the text. She squeezed her eyes shut, thinking of her father's complaints and criticisms, her mother's quick scampering attempts to fix what wasn't broken. Thinking of Lila folding her clothes, petting her hair, offering her help like Birdie deserved it.

Birdie opened her eyes, and a small shock went through her. A dog—a black-and-white border collie, its tail unwagging, its gaze fixed on Birdie—stood stock-still next to the freshly mowed family cemetery. Behind it, wind rustled the thick foliage of ferns and maples at the forest's edge. After a moment, Birdie raised her phone, took a picture of the dog with the tombstones cropped out, and sent it to Lila. *look im making new friends.*

When she looked up, the dog was still watching her. The back of her neck prickled. Was it sick? If it was, she was pretty sure that she shouldn't run—it would make the dog think she was a rabbit or something.

The dog raised one paw and took a deliberate step towards her. Then another. Birdie backed up. She'd seen tourists' dogs in the meadow before. They went nuts, bounding in and out of sight, spinning in overjoyed circles. This dog cut a slow, straight line through the grass to Birdie, trotting like one of those uber-civilized animals at Westminster.

"Back off," Birdie said, her voice too high to be threatening.

But the dog passed her without even stopping to sniff her shoes. It continued its restrained pace towards the house, mouth closed primly, fluffy tail just brushing the ground behind it. Birdie followed. "Hey, doggie?"

Its ears pointed forward. Birdie couldn't see a collar around its neck. Whenever she tried to get closer, the dog swerved or sped up.

They walked together—to an outside observer, it would have passed for together, Birdie thought, even though it was actually weird as hell—all the way to the house, where the dog wriggled beneath the porch's wood latticework.

"Christ," Birdie groaned. What if it died under there. What if it had hidden puppies under there. What if it had hidden puppies, and then *they* died. She lay on her stomach and pointed her phone's flashlight through the small gap, squinting into the murk.

For a moment, the dog's hunched outline caught the light, its eyes shining a flat green. Then, it slunk into a hole in the foundation, a pitch-black spot where the stones gleamed wet and irregular, like teeth around a gaping mouth. Its white tail tip slipped into the void.

Birdie's phone vibrated, too loud.

Aw, what a sweet puppy! Can they be my friend too?

Birdie stared into the dark. Her flashlight beam trembled. Behind her, the first tourists' cars crunched to a stop. She got up, put her phone in her pocket. She still needed to change her shirt.

Houses and children are very alike. Both constructed for a purpose: houses for shelter and warmth and a lovely view of the world outside, children for adoration and extra hands and a revival of the family name. Both expect-

ed to be vessels: of family heirlooms and furniture or of knowledge, of values. Neither are free creatures—without care, they will fall to leprous mold, rotten sores—and so both display devoted gratitude for their pale reflection of God, by whose mercy they endure and grow.

The House knows this the way a south wall knows sunlight and a north wall knows moss and dissolution. In the natural way of the no-longer-living, like the intelligence of tossed knucklebones. The House cherishes its family with a long memory.

Because houses and children share their souls, a haunted house loves a child the way dying dogs love the damp twilight beneath porches. Simple recognition, like to like. So it has been for all the House's years that a startled and wayward Daughter—never a Son, except for once and by accident—will find her gaze turning to the abyss of an opened door, and she will sense her kindred there.

So it was with the Victorian Daughter, whose Father built her a hanging garden of dollhouses. The Victorian Daughter who, despite her many fine examples for well-spun households, found herself fantasizing about a stranger, softer home, filled with angels. Her dreams so troubled her that she attempted to pass them to a dear friend by way of a kiss, their skirts rustling in the horrible silence. Not long after, in the basement, she tried her hand at an exorcism by way of small cuts. Her blood touched the stones—Sister to Sister—and she beheld the House as she had never known it, and she shared its haunting for the rest of her maiden days.

Most children, of course, eventually commit the original sin of leaving home, as is necessary for their later return and salvation. The newest Daughter has returned, but she has never been saved. She directed her love outward, to *wicked and undeserving types. Petty, townish girls. The Father was right to turn them away, to plead with the Daughter to look inward for the strength that eluded her.*

The House had not hoped for change, as hope is irrelevant to shifting daylight and passing seasons, but the House kept its records of other reformations, of children like mad dogs who bit the hands of their masters, only to return contrite and obedient years later. The newest Daughter's Father wears his own penance like a gift, a holy order of grief. He stands by his Father's tombstone. But his child—she plans to run away again even as she steps through the front door. She shivers. Someone is walking over her grave, she thinks. She is almost correct, but before she can comprehend the truth of the matter, her mind returns to dreams of flight.

Houses have their virtue over children in this regard, for houses, even haunted ones, do not dream.

In the third-floor hallway, Birdie caught her mom's arm. The string of tourists behind the tall daughter shuffled to a stop, peering at tiny rolling pins and kerchief bedspreads while Birdie whispered to her mom.

"Mom, there's a dog under the porch."

"Oh, yes." Her mom had covered up the Band-Aid on her forehead with a wide 1960s-style headband. She waved at a little girl clutching a stuffed rabbit. "They come around sometimes. It's why the neighbors asked for help when they lost their poor pooches."

"I think it went into the foundation?" Birdie ignored a tourist tapping her hard on the shoulder, asking about the provenance of a particular doll dress. She also ignored the fact that they didn't really have neighbors. The closest house was miles away. "It was acting weird."

"How about when we're done with the day, we check the basement together?"

"I'm not going into the basement," Birdie snapped.

Her mom's eyes cut to the guests, whose cell cameras clicked and clicked.

"Let's talk about it later," her mom said, patting her cheek. Beneath a charm bracelet jingling with a decade's worth of Mother's Days peeked a blue-green bruise. Birdie's breath caught—she'd seen those marks on her own wrist, heard her mother fret about how Birdie "just marked easily," felt the fury in her father's grip as he dragged her, six years old and sobbing, from the basement where she'd made a mess of his work. She'd jostled his arm while he painted a pink-ribboned daughter doll. But her father had never laid hands on her mom before—had he?

If Birdie's mother saw anything in her daughter's face, she ignored it. "Just focus on the tour for now."

She wove away through the murmuring tourists. Birdie stared at their faces, at their happy expectation. None of them had noticed her mother's injury. She inhaled deeply. "Okay! Who wants to see my bedroom?"

A few minutes later, tourists leaned over her desk and bed to examine miniature reproductions of white picket dreams. All Birdie's actual furniture was low to the ground to make more room for the exhibits. If she wanted a book from her shelf, she had to crawl along the floor. And when she stood up, she needed to watch her head, since the dioramas in her bedroom stretched wide and deep, the better to show off suburban yards populated with tiny mailboxes and neat Victory Gardens and artfully discarded bicycles with piano-wire spokes. They jutted out over Birdie, looming as though to make sure she was really asleep in bed, that she was really doing her geometry work, that she was only looking up pictures of girls online for fashion advice.

Birdie stood with her arms crossed in front of the closet. It was the one place without dolls—though her father had tried to install a miniature fashion exhibit when Birdie was nine, and she'd cried until her mom had volunteered her sewing corner instead. In any case, she didn't need anyone poking through it, even if she had taken most of her contraband with her the night she ran away.

Rabbit Plushie Girl sat on Birdie's quilted bed, her gaze wandering the walls, her mouth slightly open. This kind of kid was her parents' favorite tourist, the kind who made her father's chest puff out by telling Birdie, "You're so lucky." Birdie once despaired of ever being as beloved as those girls. Later, she just hated them.

Birdie palmed her phone, checking for new messages from Lila. Her thumb hovered over the keyboard, typing and deleting, typing and deleting.

i think my dad is hurting my mom
glad i only have to be here for a few more days lol
somethings wrong with that dog i sent you a picture of
wish you were here. not. wouldnt wish that on anyone lolol

She was still trying to find the right words at the tour's end, up in the attic with the vintage Barbie Dreamhouses. The pink mansions crowding the floor and walls broke enough sightlines that she could huddle in a corner.

can i call? things are weird.
i wish you were here.

Finally, she set a blonde and a brunette Barbie in bed together, took a picture, and sent it to Lila, which was basically the same thing as talking about her feelings. She caught sight of Lila's reply—a keyboard smash of every available heart emoji—before a tourist rounded the corner. "*There* you are!"

Birdie shoved her phone out of sight reflexively, and the tourist's thin smile tightened. "Bridget? Your mother was *so* excited to tell everyone about your visit, so I came to say hello. You and my daughter went to school together." She came even closer. "Mary Katherine? You remember."

She remembered. Birdie's skin flushed and then froze as she stared down at the woman's lined face. Traces of Birdie's ex-girlfriend lingered in the mother's sharp brows and narrow jaw. Birdie had seen that jaw catch starlight like its own crescent moon so many times when she'd snuck out to meet M.K. Taylor in the woods. Her eyes flicked to the window over the woman's shoulder, as though she'd be able to see her old girlfriend's headlights blinking on and off through the summer trees, huge cryptid fireflies. M.K.'s mother cleared her throat.

"Um," Birdie said. "Yeah. How is she?"

"She doesn't call enough." Mrs. Taylor moved forward, and Birdie stepped back, bumping the Dreamhouse and rattling the trysting Barbies behind her. "Maybe you can tell me how she is? Since you two were *such good friends.*"

She spat the last words. A few other tourists were glancing at them now from among the pink labyrinth. Rabbit Plushie Girl's big eyes flicked between Mrs. Taylor and Birdie as she squeezed the bunny close. Birdie's limbs stiffened, seemed to fuse. The scent of warm plastic spiked. This woman—this woman who hated her—had just been inside Birdie's childhood bedroom.

Birdie became aware of an apologetic smile fixed on her face. She was supposed to do something.

Mrs. Taylor's narrowed eyes slid to the two Barbies in bed, and she reached past Birdie to pluck the brunette free, taking in its pink, satin-nightgowned form, then staring up at Birdie with disgust wrinkling her features.

Actually, fuck this.

Feeling surged back into Birdie's hands, and she snatched the doll from Mrs. Taylor, holding it close to her chest. "Maybe your daughter doesn't feel like dealing—"

The lights flickered.

Birdie flinched, gasping along with the other guests. Her gaze shot to the hatch. Her mother waited there, delicate hand poised over the wall's light switch, blue eyes alight with silent pleas to her daughter as she laughed and apologized to the tourists.

After Birdie's bruised wrist healed and she'd started avoiding the basement, the only dolls she could count on playing with were Barbies. Dad didn't like them as much. Her mom had walked in on seven-year-old Birdie kissing a Barbie's tiny head, and although she hadn't said anything bad—hadn't said anything at all—there had been something troubled lurking at the edges of her mouth and eyes, like a glimpse of skin beneath a mask.

Mrs. Taylor had jumped when the lights went out, but now she glared at Birdie again. "Maybe my daughter *what*?" she hissed.

Birdie swallowed, smoothed the Barbie's long brunette hair. "I'm sure Mary Katherine is just busy." She pulled a smile onto her face like she was operating machinery. "Please don't touch the exhibits."

Mrs. Taylor opened and closed her fists several times before whirling around and heading for the exit. Birdie's mom helped Rabbit Plushie Girl find her footing, then followed her down the ladder without another glance at her daughter.

Birdie set the doll in the purple armchair next to the Dreamhouse's bed. Maybe she should put the blonde doll in the walk-in closet and take another picture for Lila. And why stop there? Maybe she could do something even more pathetic, even more self-pitying. So she readied herself to take the tourists down to the gift shop instead.

———

The Mother knew early on of the Daughter's strange affinities and did little to discourage them. True, the Mother sewed a pink gingham dress with eyelet lace, gifted heart-shaped lockets, and tied apron strings double-knotted round the Daughter's waist at Christmas. But what of it? The Daughter left the dress crumpled in her closet and ran wild and barelegged and muddy, laid an iridescent beetle corpse in the locket where a curl of beloved hair was meant to rest, fidgeted free from the apron like an untrained mutt that couldn't abide its collar. The Daughter's eyes fixed on female guests as though they were holy visitors with star-tipped wings. The Mother did not do enough to amend the girl. So often the rod was left in the Father's hands: to scold the Daughter, to soften her callused fists with pretty work, to set her on the right path once more.

The Family holds together the House, and the House holds together the Family, and if either of them flew free from their orbit, then the roof would crack from the house and soar into the sky, and the windows would shatter and glass would fly like birds, and the walls would splinter into cloudborne flotsam, and the doors would never close again, and the beds and the chairs and the tables would furnish some new heaven, and the Daughter would forget the name of her Father's Father's Father, and the dolls—

And all the dolls would go, leave their front doors unlocked, and glide over the New England towns into eternity.

To prevent this ungodly apocalypse, this end of days where the rest of the world lives on in ignorance of its loss, the Father has tried to hold his Family close. And even with all his teaching, the Daughter has dropped his hand and fled.

The Daughter now dreams of the House closing in upon her. Yet one night, years ago, the Daughter woke to find that she'd rediscovered her earliest memory of her Father. He'd lifted her above his head, staring up at her with the same expression she later saw him direct at a solar eclipse—unnerved, awed, wondering if it was truly safe to look. His thick glasses shone over his gray eyes, but his hands clutched her beneath her armpits—too tightly, in her memory, driving her overall buttons into her toddler chest. She squirmed. He nearly dropped her, then set her on the ground and dusted his hands.

After remembering all this, the Daughter lay in bed with her face wet and her breath catching in her throat, wondering why he'd been so relieved to let go of her. So foolish. The Father was never the one who let go.

—————

Birdie felt lost inside herself until dinnertime, when she blinked back into her body while holding a wooden tray that her mom heaped with food. A bowl of tomato soup sent up curls of basil-fragrant steam next to a plate stacked with tiny triangles of grilled cheese (cheddar, Swiss, pepper jack). She didn't remember helping to make them, but the countertops were thick with pots and pans bumping up against acrylic-boxed displays of the same tools in miniature.

"So there were some challenging guests today?" her mom asked, rearranging the sandwiches into a sunburst pattern.

"Yeah." Her throat was raw from speaking so much.

"Say 'yes,' sweetie. Mrs. Taylor complained about you being on your phone," her mom continued, now trying out a pyramid structure for the sandwiches, "But I told her *to her face* that she was a liar. You wouldn't be so unprofessional. Was her daughter one of your special friends?"

Birdie twitched. Girlfriend. She could just say *girlfriend*. But her mom had defended her, so she stayed quiet.

Her mom hummed and dusted crumbs from her fingers. "I did notice you texting someone in the meadow. And at one point on the tour, which you shouldn't do next time. Are you seeing anyone?"

Had Birdie's mother been watching her the whole time? From the many shelves, tiny painted eyes glittered. The dolls pursued their endless tasks, caught in a limbo before mealtime. Birdie stared down to avoid their joyful purgatory. Under her mother's well-manicured fingers, the sandwiches formed a fan. A smiley face. The letter B. Birdie's arms strained from holding the tray steady. The soup trembled. Her soles felt like pounded meat in her thin sneakers.

"I'm dating a woman." Birdie shifted back a half-step towards the bright dining room. "So, I'm seeing her, yeah."

"'*Yes.*' You could have brought her, you know. Your father's gotten much better about it."

Birdie's father had walked in on her and her first girlfriend in the kitchen, their hands linked, their lips both tasting like the lemonade Birdie had just drunk. His rage had flooded scarlet up his neck—but his eyes had flicked to the gift shop, checking that it was empty, before he started yelling.

This isn't what a good daughter does.

Was it that she loved girls, or was it that he hadn't guessed this about her?

"Could we just talk about the dog instead?" Birdie asked. Her mom, satisfied with the sandwiches or maybe sensing Birdie's flight response, moved on to add a tall glass of ice water to the tray.

"Soon." A side salad in a leaded glass bowl slid next to Birdie's forearm, halved cherry tomatoes glinting. "What's her name? You could still invite her."

"I'm not asking her to come to a house where she might get mauled by a sick dog." Birdie snapped, then bit her tongue. Her mom, bent over the deep pot of soup, did not respond apart from a sharp intake of breath, and Birdie may have imagined that too—her mother hadn't moved, hadn't blinked, hadn't even glanced at her.

The outdoors' evening orchestra—branches, bugs, furry critters in the grass—murmured through the closed kitchen window. Birdie locked her elbows and waited.

Second portions of everything followed. Birdie's biceps burned under the weight, and she held the tray as far from her borrowed white poplin blouse as possible. She hadn't had time to change back into her skull shirt once the last tourists left.

"I don't think Dad can eat all this," she said, interrupting the cricket song that had filled the silence between mother and daughter.

"Oh, I know." Her mom picked up a second, smaller tray snuggled next to an exhibit of mother dolls beside their antique stoves, beehive ovens, fire-bubbled cauldrons. Her gray hair, pulled back in a smooth bun, shone as if silvered onto her scalp. "It's for me as well. And you. We thought it would be nice to eat together as a family tonight."

Birdie took a deep, basil-scented breath. "In the dining room?"

"Well, no." Her mother's smile crooked up without touching her eyes. "Your father has to work, and the stairs are quite steep, so..."

Her blue gaze slid to the basement door. Birdie set down the tray, silverware clattering. A pigtailed girl doll with a plate of cookies toppled over above her.

"No."

Beneath her frilly apron, her mother's shoulders drooped. "Just one night. It's not a big ask, Bridget—"

"Yes, it is." Birdie's voice rose. "You know that. Is he making you do this?"

"Bridget." Her mother's voice was stern, wounded, and Birdie's stomach shriveled. "Your father doesn't *make me* do anything."

"Right." Birdie wrapped her arms around herself. "He doesn't need to make you. He just asks, and you do it."

"You can ask too, you know." Her mom set down the smaller tray and reached for Birdie's forearm, the yellow stove light turning her smooth palm waxy. Her charm bracelet tinkled. The bruise beneath it was silent.

Birdie could ask.

Are you happy?

Is he hurting you?

When I ran away, do you wish that I'd taken you with me?

She stared at her mom, who was so still that she seemed not to be breathing.

Why do you always choose him?

Something pressed up behind her mother's shining eyes like a shadow moving behind illuminated curtains. She didn't blink. Birdie swallowed.

"I'm not going into the basement." Her voice wavered.

Her mother sprang back into motion: hands on hips, huff-puff of breath. Next to the vintage gas stove and gleaming copper pans, she could have been any nice old lady whose child had just stolen from the cookie jar. A real Rockwell moment. "So you're going to make me carry this heavy thing down on my own?"

Birdie grabbed a plate of sandwiches. "Ask Dad to help you."

Birdie's mother sighed and hefted the tray, unsteady under its weight. Steaming soup cascaded over her thumb, and Birdie reached towards the scalded flesh as if she could stop what had already happened.

Her mother's coral lips curved up in a gracious smile. Behind her, the wall crawled with little motionless mothers in their own dim kitchens.

"Don't worry, Bridget," her mother said. What was that in her eyes? "It doesn't hurt anymore."

She disappeared through the narrow door, her footsteps growing softer down the basement stairs. Birdie stared into the unlit gap, listened to her father's creaking murmurs, the voice of a forgotten and resentful creature. *Where is...but she...*

And when the shouting started, Birdie fled upstairs on childhood instinct, her heart frantic, her guilt a collar cinched tight.

———

The Daughter's memory was profoundly scattered, a trail of messy crumbs across a clean tablecloth. She flinched at any raised voice, cringed through time at the sight of an unfortunate chair, whirled through the House with glamoured eyes, seeing only a ruin of love. Fool. The House remembered better.

When the Daughter was five and eating breakfast in the dining room, the Father placed his hands over the Mother's eyes as she cleaned, and she laughed. He dropped a necklace around the Mother's neck, kissed her cheek while the Daughter watched. The air smelled of lilacs from the open window, vanilla from her mother's perfume, woody dust from the houses that needed wiping down. The Daughter's short legs kicked the air—she hadn't yet become a lanky horror making half-hearted overtures toward womanhood—and her blue gaze was inattentive. She didn't know that, a decade and a half before, the Father had carried the Mother, laughing, over the threshold. She didn't know how they had hoped and struggled and sacrificed for children, how many wished-for babies had vanished before growing any larger than the smallest dolls, how the Father had cradled the weeping Mother. The Daughter never cared to know, and she only remembered the Mother's smile drooping as the Father moved away, and the Mother polishing the dust off a grinning family's sculpted meal.

When the Daughter was eleven and wandering the house, somehow unable to discover anything useful to do, she turned a corner and found the Father on his tiptoes in the hall, peering like a child into one of the out-of-the-way dioramas. She ducked out of sight. He murmured: Sure, it's lonely, but you have each other. That's always been enough before. *The Daughter sat against the dimly lit wall, listening to his gentle tones rise and fall out of hearing. Her shoulders loosened, and the summer warmth and the Father's soft voice fell over her like a blanket, and she slept. She never thought of this when she walked by that lonely dollhouse, but she marked every doll that had ever watched her in her minor crises (the scolding, the sobbing). She remembers the forlorn face of every doll the Father commanded her to look at, so close her nose spotted grease on their paint: see the dust, the spiderweb, the dead spider, the desiccated egg sac, everything she had missed while cleaning. She found the Father in all things, so long as they were painful.*

And when the Daughter was seventeen and discovered a dog hit on the road, howling, and she begged the Mother and Father for help, she never recalled the Mother pulling her aside in a shielding embrace. She didn't choose to remember the special plot dug deep next to the family graveyard's wrought-iron fence, nor the body wrapped in bright fabric, nor the sweet-scented daffodils and hyacinths that marked its place, the ones that the Mother kneeled to plant. She only saw, again and again, the hazel bulge of the dog's eyes, the way they fixed on hers with their pooled-open pupils. She only heard the whoosh-thunk *of the Father swinging the shovel. She hadn't visited the grave in years. She hadn't even noticed it was empty.*

The Daughter shook herself to pieces over these measly, tragic crumbs. But if the House had fingers—if the House blasphemed thus—then the House would have licked each thumbprint, pressed them to every pathetic scrap, and devoured those morsels in an ecstasy of teeth and tongue. The House remembered what it was to be hungry, because the House was still starving.

———

Like Birdie always did when things were bad, she ate in the tower, perched halfway up the spiral staircase. Around her hung objects that shouldn't have been homes but were anyway: a stack of books, a computer monitor, a wine bottle. In a nearby violin, a mouse mother brought cookies to her mouse children as they practiced piano and cello. The rodent father was nowhere in sight. Good. Birdie munched her tiny sandwiches, crunching through the buttery grilled crust, dragging out long strings of gooey cheese, scattering crumbs. If her father was still yelling, she couldn't hear it.

If her mom was in trouble, she couldn't hear that either.

A glimpse of movement. Birdie half-stood, ready to rush up the stairs and lock the tower door behind her— but it was just a dog traipsing through the grass outside, the same black-and-white one as before. It walked past the narrow tower window and vanished.

Past the woods, the sky faded from vivid clementine to lilac. Lila was precise about these shades. When she'd first suggested moving in together, she'd told Birdie: "I'd be great at interior decorating," and the selling point— because that's what it was, a selling point—broke Birdie's heart a little. It was the kind of pitch she imagined her mom making to her dad. *I can sew all the doll clothes, and I make great food! I keep smiling no matter what.*

Another dog padded by.

Birdie sat up. This one was tan with brown ears, some kind of lanky shepherd mix. It passed out of sight, but Birdie kept her eyes on the glass, trying to stare past her own ghostly reflection.

Third dog. Small. Floppy ginger ears.

Fourth dog. Old pit bull, walking with a limp.

Fifth. Golden retriever.

They all paced the same circuit, their noses to the ground. Birdie put down her sandwich, her mouth dry. She knew those dogs. She'd stapled flyers next to their furry faces and stared into their grinning, know-nothing eyes. Her hands trembled.

She made herself look from tiny house to tiny house. The wine bottle had a nautical theme, complete with itty-bitty cable-knit sweaters on the dolls. The hollow stack of novels had other bookshelves inside it, and Birdie knew that if she leaned over the railing far enough, she'd be able to smell the old paper. The computer monitor, acquired from a private collector, was a diorama of *The Matrix*. Morpheus offered Neo the pills. She shouldn't worry about the dogs. They could be other dogs. And anyway, they were gone now.

Birdie's eyes flicked to the window.

The porch lamps made their eyes shine green.

Just beyond the ring of light, the five dogs sat together in an identical prim posture. Their heads tilted up at the window. Their eyes fixed on Birdie.

"What the *fuck*?" She scrambled to her feet, nearly dropping the plate of sandwiches to the floor far below. The dogs stood up as one.

Iron steps clanged beneath her feet as Birdie rushed up the tightly spiraling stairs and—old habits—locked the tower door behind her. There were no windows in the long hallway that led to her bedroom, and even the dolls seemed blind in the dark, but Birdie still hunched her shoulders like it would shake off some unknown watcher.

In her room, she closed the curtains, turned off the lights. She huddled in her bed with her knees under her chin. Which noises were the wind through the trees, and which were dogs creeping through the meadow? Which was the house creaking into its foundations, and which was her father's footstep on the stairs?

For a long time, she sat in the dark while nothing happened. A part of her knew that if she did nothing long enough, someone else would act for her—so, when the lock in her door *clunked* into place, Birdie barely flinched. She swung her legs out of bed like her mom had called her for breakfast and crossed to the bedroom door. In the illuminated gap beneath, no shadows waited. Whoever had locked it—her father, probably—had already moved on.

All the doors in the house locked from the outside and inside. A necessity of museums and shitty parents. Birdie turned the old key, its lacy iron cold against her fingers, and slid the deadbolt free with a whisper of metal on metal.

The key twisted, grinding against her skin. The lock slammed into place. Birdie jerked back, her yelp ringing through the air even as she slapped her palms over her mouth. Her shadowy room drew close as a hot breath against her ear. Among the doll families, another awareness pressed in.

Birdie strained to hear anything beneath the silence. "Mom?" she whispered to the door. No one answered. Birdie hugged her arms across her chest. "Dad?"

Nothing.

After a few moments, she stretched a hand out to the key again, but it crushed itself into place, refused to move.

Nothing broke the light beneath the door. No one outside. On the shelves, doll eyes glittered. Birdie grabbed a pillow and a blanket and fled to the closet, putting another door between herself and whatever lay outside, giving herself shit even as she huddled under her musty, unworn clothes.

The doorknob was old, like everything in the house, so it was just getting jammed in the summer heat. And the dogs had just smelled her food through an open window. And her mom had just forgotten about the basement stuff. She'd forgotten what the basement meant to Birdie, and that was the kindest explanation.

If she'd only forgotten the worst of it, Birdie would have understood, but it seemed like her mother had erased *everything*. Her mother had forgotten that after her husband found fourteen-year-old Birdie kissing a girlfriend, Birdie worked in the basement for the rest of the summer, breathing in the eternal, slightly metallic mold stench that haunted the tricentennial stones. She had grown paler and more ghoulish every day while the house's unseen eyes bore down on the back of her neck. Moving items into boxes. Cataloguing their contents. Ensuring no rot had spread to each hidden-away family. The great preservation of her heritage never ended. Behind and beneath the archival coffins, detritus of once-perfect homes accumulated, paper dolls spotted with mold and half-dead spiders, tiny furniture gnawed away by pests and rot. Once, Birdie found a dead mouse curled around a dollhouse vanity, its sparse gray hide mummified tight across its skull and ribs.

Across the room, Birdie's father toiled at his own endless projects, and if his daughter coughed, or stared at the basement door, or flinched at the sight of a rodent's corpse, he raised his brass jeweler's loupe and asked, "Tired already?"

It's just until school starts again, Birdie had told herself every night at dinner, as her mom dished out homemade cherry ice cream that tasted like lost sunshine. Her mom gave her extra, squeezed her shoulder, reassured Birdie in private that, yes, it was only for the summer.

But then the next summer came, and the next, and the basement was always waiting, and the weight of the house above grew heavier and heavier until Birdie just wished the whole thing would collapse atop her. Until Birdie felt it was fate to be buried beneath it. Until even her girlfriends accepted that no, she couldn't come to the coast, and she couldn't go for ice cream, and she couldn't even see them while the sun was out. Rendezvousing with her after dusk, as though Birdie were a creature of the night, became normal. In the dark, none of her explanations made sense. "I get it," they said at first, their eye-rolls a quick gleam in their shadowy front seats, "My dad is really weird too." And then, later: "I mean, you're going to take over the museum someday, right? This is, like, training. A summer job." And, finally: "You could just say that you don't want to see me anymore."

Just until the end of summer. And now, just four more days. Just four more days. Birdie's eyes burned, and she swiped at them. Her heart was a wrung-out rag. She pulled out her phone.

li, she typed, *things are weird.*

She nibbled her lip. Deleted it. Retyped it. Hit send before she could change her mind.

Her phone started buzzing in her hand. Birdie answered and burst into tears.

———

The House remembered this Daughter first for her clear eyes and second for her lying. The House recalled her willingness to press her ears to doors she'd locked with her own hands, her breath fanning across the walls; her daring leaps from her window, her forearms and calves scraping bloody against the walnut tree's branches; her ecstatic flight through the meadow, a disobedient beast beneath the milk-rivered sky. In later years, embracing shadows waited at the forest's edge, or headlights flared like witches' lamps. The Daughter lost herself in the thick foliage. Returned with her hair cut ragged and short, returned with her lips kissed red, returned with a swagger like a man's.

But the House could not forget how that defiant truth shrank to almost nothing in the Daughter afterwards, to a muttered "I don't know," when her parents asked about the scabs on her knees and elbows, to a snapped "I just wanted to," when she'd reduced her long braid to wispy, boyish locks, to whines and crying when her Father's voice echoed off the ceilings like God's thunder. Whether she was six or sixteen, she cried just the same.

When she finally ran away, the Daughter did not leave quietly, another sin. She screamed. Opened the interior of the House as one would open a wound. She bled the family in full view of an outsider. Shameful. She cried at the top of the stairs, saltwater pattering the floor. At the front door where the Father had once confessed his love, he now apologized again and again to a stranger, a police officer, who did not deserve it and did not care. The Daughter tore new holes in everything. Wet, black mold. Blind, crawling termite. Shivering mouse in the walls. Barely a Daughter at all.

It would not have been so difficult to admit the truth, to honor her parents, to smile. To stay in her bed, in the House, in a state of simple grace. To stop crying.

How unsurprising that she cried even when speaking to one who supposedly loved her. In the closet, the Daughter held the phone as though embracing it and cried to her friend without words, and her friend told her: come home, come home, come home. *The Daughter agreed, not realizing that she already was home.*

Her Father had never cried so much, even when welts rose on his thighs and he clenched his hands into fists, even when his youthful flesh trembled and he craved honey until sickness. He knew what was asked of him. When he left the House, he whispered I love you to the front door, just as the Victorian Daughter did. He always knew that he was walking a long circle, striding the wildest edges of the world he had earned before resting, relieved, at its center. When he left, he thought of everyone inside, waiting for his return.

And where did the Father go during his long days in the wilderness? Nowhere he cared to go back to. That's all that really needs to be said.

But she had never learned to stop running. She'd never learned to be a good Daughter. To turn her eyes to scraps of sky between rotting straw, to trust herself to a wisdom bitter as starvation, to grant forgiveness even as the snow on her tongue did not melt. To love the hand beneath hers on the knife. No, the newest Daughter had not yet learned.

The House clicked shut its locks once more.

————

At breakfast the next morning, Birdie pushed scrambled eggs around her plate until her mom sat across from her. It was easier to speak on an empty stomach. "Mom, I have to leave early."

Her mother's face froze in a half-smile, her blue eyes focused somewhere past Birdie's ear. The breakfast nook was crowded with shelves of little blonde families settling down to eat in farmhouses, their heads bowed as they said grace. They seemed to be praying for something else now. A few moments of complete, house-empty stillness held themselves in the air. Something moved in the basement.

And Birdie's mother reached for the salt. "What happened, sweetie?"

Birdie shrugged, remembering Lila's voice, fierce through the phone. *You can just leave. Just go.* But it felt wrong to say nothing. "Just some stuff came up."

"What kind?" Her mother shook a few grains of salt over her eggs, then continued: "We were counting on you."

"I know, but—" Birdie held her knees under the table. The smell of fried potatoes and eggs turned her stomach. "You said there wouldn't be guests, and then there were, and the basement stuff—"

"You're leaving early because of one day with guests?" Her mother's tone carried a cheerful lilt even in confusion, even in anger.

Birdie kept her eye on the vase of wildflowers in the center of the table. Her mother woke up early to pick the meadow blooms that had barely blown open. When Birdie was younger, she'd gone with her, dashing ahead in the petal-blue dawn, clearing leaves and moss from generations of stones in the family grave plot, returning to her mother's side to check that neither of them had become ghosts.

She dug her fingernails into her kneecaps. "Are there going to be guests again today?"

Her mother sighed. "I was planning on helping your father while you gave them the tour, Bridget. Because of your basement preferences. But I can lead the tour."

"I'm not—"

"Going in the basement." Her mom's gaze really met hers for the first time since Birdie had arrived, a shimmer of fury beneath their worn, peaceful blue. "You've been very clear about that with me. Would you like to let your father in on that preference? Or would you rather I be the one to pass it on for you?"

Her voice hitched on the last word, and she turned away, staring out the window into the wide meadow, where mist coiled among the grass and the distant family gravestones. Birdie watched the oil congealing on her plate.

"I'll make fresh eggs," her mother said.

"Please don't."

"I'm not having my daughter's last meal be cold eggs." Her mother swept her breakfast into the trash, her shoulders hunched. "You're right. If you feel upset or uncomfortable, then you should probably go. I was so happy to have you home again. It was good to not have it be just your father and me."

Unspoken: *If you love me, do not leave me alone with him.*

Birdie's father slammed doors after arguments. Just walked around the house slamming doors, tipping over anything in the exhibits that wasn't glued down. Once, Birdie had looked down the stairs and seen her mom kneeling among all the tiny objects that make a household feel like home, gathering them in her palm. It was too easy to imagine her mom trailing in her father's wake around the empty house, trying to make everything appear as it always had been. Without any kind of buffer from guests, without any kind of whipping girl like Birdie around, what was her father like? What was the Band-Aid on her mom's forehead and the bruise on her wrist, and if those were the parts that Birdie could see, then what injuries crept invisibly up her mom's limbs? How long until he broke her bones?

"I can stay for dinner," Birdie said. Her mom faced her, and Birdie swallowed. "I won't stay the night, but I can stay for dinner. I'll take the guests around."

Birdie's mom beamed, her face drawing up into happy and relieved wrinkles. "Oh, Bridget, that's wonderful. Thank you, sweetie."

She crossed the room to kiss Birdie's forehead and then headed for the pantry, where ceramic jars shaped like houses held drifts of flour and sugar, suffocating any occupants. "I'll make pancakes."

On the tour—stomach heavy with pancakes and syrup, dressed in another ruffled blouse her mother had lent her—Birdie took a picture of a furry gray spider inside one of the dollhouses. In the overexposed photo, the spider crouched on the stained wallpaper next to a rosy-cheeked daughter doll playing with (what else) dolls. *look at this weird dog*, she texted to Lila.

Ewww, Lila responded. A laughing emoji popped up as if to reassure Birdie. Then, a moment later: *When are you going to be home? Do you want me to cook you something?*

Shit. Birdie led the tourists through the Victorian room, the little mansions like fractal children of the main house. Her mouth shaped words from the weekend tours of her adolescence. Varied cadence, light tone, pause for giggles after the puns, march forward even if no one laughed. Years ago, an older tourist had shifted his eyes from Birdie to her father and spoken like she wasn't there. "You've got her well-trained," he said. Birdie's father had thanked him. Birdie's mother had put a hand on her shoulder. Birdie herself felt like something inside her had shrunk to almost nothing and rattled loose through her ribs. She'd stared into the attic windows of a Victorian—there it was now, the same as it always had been—and hoped to see someone looking back at her.

She typed a quick response while the tourists milled around, their faces as anonymous as any of the other dolls in the house. *im staying for dinner. dont want mom to get in trouble w dad.*

Her phone vibrated right away, even though Birdie was almost positive that Lila was at her job. *Bird, you were SOBBING last night.*

im not sleeping over ok im just helping for the day.

This isn't normal!!! Birdie!!!

im working. talk later. Birdie tucked her phone into her pocket just as a last message from Lila came up.

You're never going to let me in, are you?

Birdie said something about towers. Birdie called attention to the trims and styles. Birdie swung open a house and found a Daughter doll in the basement. Birdie pressed a hand to her sternum, hard enough to ache, as she led the way upstairs. Something had split inside. Something was crawling free.

———

The Daughter tries not to know what she knows: that the body is an early memorial to an ever-dying self. It is shaped by daily wonders and cruel accidents, just like any other home. Grief and joy meet, and kiss, just beneath the skin.

The House, for instance, knows itself in its wood and stone the way a surviving lover knows the fresh-cut marble of their beloved's tomb. It knows itself through the dents in the walls that once cradled knuckles, the creaky place outside the second-floor bedrooms where so many miscreant feet hesitated, the corner of the basement where everything went cold.

The Daughter could realize this too, if she tried. She runs her fingers over and over the silvery crescent carved into the back of her skull. She rubs at her left wrist to search for the seam of the poorly healed fracture, gained at such a cost when she fell from the rain-slick walnut tree and told no one until her teacher noticed her wincing. She scratches the bottom of her foot where she once plunged through a floorboard.

Her Father had been pleased then, for she'd crashed into a secret diorama, a souvenir from the Victorian Daughter once her mind had clouded around her one remaining desire: to build, and build, and build. The Father had held the newest Daughter's small ankle, his grip tight but confusingly gentle, and worked a silver rocking chair the size of his thumbnail out of the Daughter's heel. He set to work cleaning it while the Mother hurried her child out the door. Their car vanished into the moonless woods at speed, as though the Daughter would perish if they didn't reach the hospital. She would not have died—and she knew it—but for months afterwards, she feigned illness in the hopes of a warm hand on her forehead, her Mother's blue eyes meeting hers as they had in the car's mirror.

The Daughter would realize this if she tried: that the House's body and hers are two sisters linked in material and memory. But for now, the House knows what no one else but the Daughter can know, the comfort no one else can cherish. In the House, no one is ever home alone.

———

After the tour, Birdie closed out the ancient gift shop register, counting everything twice and then once more. She tucked the day's thin earnings into a brown and brittle envelope marked with the elaborate handwriting of a great-aunt who had died ages ago. Beside her, wooden-headed dolls dangled from their keychains as though at a gallows.

Outside, the light dipped into golden hour, casting honey-colored warmth over the meadow. A walk would be lovely. The air around her ankles would be cool and humid, already dipping into dew, and she didn't know when she'd next come back.

Probably when her dad died.

She shouldn't think about it. She shouldn't feel relieved, not when her mother would be devastated. Birdie yanked the door handle. It stuck, and she pulled again, bracing her foot against the frame. The summer-swollen wood didn't budge. She took a step back, glaring.

"It's just a walk," Birdie muttered.

As if a friend were coming, the door swung gently open. Birdie stared. The meadow rustled, but in the distance, no breeze swayed the forest treetops. A spectral fingertip nudged the borrowed cotton blouse against her back.

Birdie turned on her heel, spine straight—there was no one behind her, of course—and walked with measured steps up to her bedroom. She texted Lila. *door just opened on its own.*

Lila's response arrived a few minutes later while Birdie was shoving her clothes into her suitcase. *Wow. It's almost like you should leave.*

im packing now ok im just kinda freaked out.
Cool.

Birdie straightened up to reply. *thats not v helpful*

A quiet knock on her bedroom door was all the warning Birdie had before her mom walked in. Birdie tucked the phone behind her back. It buzzed in her hand as she and her mother exchanged smiles.

"Dinner's almost ready," her mom said. "Is everything okay?"

"Yeah, totally," Birdie said. Her phone shook, furious, against her palm. Lila hated fumbling with the keys when she was angry, preferred a phone call.

"Is someone calling you, sweetie?" Her mother leaned sideways, peering at the source of the repetitive *vrrrr... vrrrr...*

"No." Birdie mashed the power button repeatedly. "I mean, yeah. Telemarketer."

A small, unconvinced smile touched her mother's lips. "Well, come downstairs soon." She turned to leave, but paused at the door, her shoulders as straight as if she were hung on a coat hanger. "And Bridget, say 'yes' instead of 'yeah.' It's more polite."

Birdie stared for a moment, and her phone began buzzing again.

"Yes," Birdie said. As her mother left with nearly silent steps, Birdie declined the call. Her mother could be waiting just outside. Anything could be waiting out there.

cant talk right now, she typed. *i love you.*

She watched her phone screen. Three dots appeared, vanished, reappeared. Finally: *You're not acting like it.*

And: *Take care of yourself and LEAVE okay?*

And: *Sorry. I'm tired. Gonna go lie down.*

And Birdie stared at the screen, waiting. And no messages popped up. And Lila didn't say *I love you* back.

Birdie went down to dinner.

At the dining room table—just her and her mom, just like it had been since she'd arrived—her silent phone weighed heavy in her shirt pocket. She kept reminding herself to sit tall, taller, as if her Lurch-esque stature had ever contributed to an evening of sparkling conversation. She made a respectable attempt, cutting her chicken and commenting on its tenderness, cleaning her plate like she'd been raised to do. Across the candles, her mom rearranged her food.

"Why haven't I seen Dad at all? Has he even been upstairs?" Another attempt, a two-for-one: small talk, plus bonus interest in her father.

"He's just really busy." Her mother set down her fork, the same polite but disbelieving smile on her face as earlier. Surely she had more expressions than this. When Birdie had been very young, she'd filled a photo album with shots of herself and her mom mugging for the camera: stretching their mouths, crossing their eyes, making kissy faces. "He gets so attached to his work."

Before Birdie could ask anything else, her mom retreated to the kitchen and returned with fine china bowls and a sparkling serving dish heaped with home-made cherry ice cream. The special treat after Birdie's summer basement duties. At picnics, when Birdie and Lila dug their spoons into a shared pint of Cherry Garcia—would she get a chance to do that again?—it had never managed to be as vividly tart, as coldly sweet. Her mom's smile took on a genuine, rueful twist. "Take as much as you want. I know it's your favorite."

Birdie reached for the dish. Deep crimson syrup rippled through vanilla ice cream, looping around half-buried chunks of cherry. With her mother's hands outstretched, Birdie caught sight once again of the smudged bruise on her wrist, fully revealed in the absence of charm bracelets. It definitely looked like a thumbprint. And farther up her forearm, peeking out of her lacy sleeve—the indigo shadows of a fierce grip, livid against her mother's colorless skin.

Birdie swallowed and set the ice cream on the table. For a second, she thought she might throw up, but it was just words pushing up her throat. She was just shit at talking to her mom about anything important. She'd probably always be shit at it.

"How'd you get that bruise on your wrist?" She spoke just above a whisper. Someone was always listening. Her mother sighed, stood, heaped ice cream into the gilt-edged bowl beside Birdie.

"I fell," she said, firmly.

"That's a handprint."

"I fell, and your father caught me."

"Did he catch you after he pushed you?"

Her mother went very still. Her glassy blue eyes, fixed somewhere on the tabletop, didn't blink. Her breath hitched on an inhale and stopped.

"Mom?" Birdie grabbed her shoulder. If she was having a heart attack, she'd fall down, wouldn't she?

A woman's sobs echoed thinly through the dining room. Birdie stood up, throwing an arm over her mother's shoulders, her head whipping around. The room wobbled in her vision. She held onto her chair.

"I'm sorry," Birdie's mother said brightly, straightening from under her daughter's arm. Her skin was like threadbare cloth.

"Did you hear that?" Birdie asked.

"It's not important." Her mother laid her cool palm against Birdie's cheek, tucked Birdie's unruly hair behind her ear. "Bridget—Birdie—I'm sorry that I didn't protect you. I'm so sorry, sweetheart."

Birdie leaned into her mom's hand, her throat tightening and tightening as she struggled with the perfect way to say it. *Come with me. You deserve to leave. I'm so sorry that I left you here.*

Run.

"You can come with me," Birdie said. "We can go right now."

Her mom's face was immobile, her gaze unfocused. "Maybe," she said, and then, more strongly, "Maybe. Yes." Her blue eyes found Birdie's. She smiled.

Birdie's muscles relaxed. That was it? That was all she had to do? "Okay." She backed up, stumbling a little. "Okay, you pack some things, and I'll grab my stuff."

The ice cream melted, untouched, as she ran from the room. Maybe she could ask her mom to make some for them—her, Lila, and Birdie—to share together. Maybe everything could be okay. God, she'd never come back here again.

At the top of the stairs, Birdie staggered. The antique rug's floral design rippled beneath her feet. She tripped. A cold thrill lanced through her, immediately swallowed by numb warmth. *No.* Birdie crawled towards her bedroom, reaching for her phone. Her fingers fumbled with the lock screen as it slid in and out of focus. She heaved.

Somehow, she called Lila. Sprawled on her side across her vomit-splattered bedroom rug, Birdie listened to a tinny recording ring and ring. *Hiya, it's Lila, leave a message.*

Birdie tried to speak, her tongue touching the words she needed, and then the soft beyond embraced her.

The Mother follows the Daughter upstairs, watching smooth-faced as the girl slumps on the floor, as the lights go off throughout the House. From the Daughter's rocking chair, the Mother surveys the Daughter's chest rising and falling in an easy rhythm, the same as it did when she was just a baby in her crib, and she paces her rocking in time to the Daughter's breaths. Doors close and the locks click, but the Mother keeps her eyes on her Daughter.

Watching. It is a habit of Mothers in the House. It should make them the House's natural love, an outward embodiment of every Household instinct, but, alas, it only makes them redundant. They lack the appropriate devotion: they arrive carrying the dust of other houses, and they doubt the House and its Father, no matter how many placid smiles stretch their faces. Their memories do not recognize the scent of the House as "home." The Mother before this one neglected to bear a Daughter; this Mother neglected to bear a Son, which is worse.

On the sick-soaked rug, the Daughter's phone trembles. The Mother plucks it from the bile, her mouth unmoving as she reads the name behind the glass. With a glance at the girl's slack and restless face, the Mother declines to answer and presses her Daughter's thumb to the phone. She listens to the captured message from the Daughter's friend. Her face is a pamphlet's illustration, unmoving and simple.

The House is old, but the House understands the Mother's actions when she taps against the machine, hits "Block," hits "Delete." Beside her, a lamp flickers, and the Mother freezes. She speaks without moving her lips. "Dearest?"

A hum and blinding burst of light. Crystalline tinkling as the bulb pops. The Mother cries out into the darkness and raises her arms to her face, though her reflective eyes do not blink.

After a moment, she ceases cowering. "No—it's just you, isn't it?"

Just *you*. The House seethes, its hate scratching against the walls like a million hands.

"I've done everything—everything *for* our Family. Let me have this. Just this. For her. Please." Her mouth moves again now. Her shoulders round in a tragic, practiced shape. "Please don't tell him about Bridget's friend."

The overhead light swells with hot illumination and shatters in a miniature thunderclap, glass spitting onto the unconscious girl. The Mother watches a thin red line bead on the Daughter's cheek, glinting in the dim amber glow cast from the hall sconces. She wipes it away, dusts sparkling shards from the girl's pale hair, and secrets her phone deep in her apron pocket. Then she proceeds with *the evening's activities, as she should have done from the start.*

The Mothers watch the House and its Father with judgment, mistaking the sublime for sinfulness. Only the House's careful study yields salvation. For that reason, the House will keep the Mother's secret—for now.

———

Birdie woke to a scuffling noise, bleary eyes already searching for the source. No tourists. No parents, either, although someone had put a blanket over her while she slept on the floor. Why was she on the—

Birdie's hand flew out across the damp rug, searching for her phone. Her head pounded as if someone were inside knocking their knuckles against her eyebrows, and her mouth was acrid and sticky. Lemony cleaning scent rose in puffs as she scrabbled at the hooked wool. Her mom must have cleaned the puke. Put the blanket over her. Which meant—Birdie struggled to sit up as the room careened around her—which meant her phone was gone. A sick calm settled over her. Of course her phone was gone. Why wouldn't it be?

After all, her mom had drugged her.

Her breath caught on a sob, and she huddled in place, shaking, burying her mouth against her knee to deaden the noise. Outside the door, all was quiet. *Okay,* she thought, pushing the heels of her hands against her stubborn tear ducts. *Okay, okay, okay.* She crawled to the moonlit window, stifling a whimper as her head throbbed, and looked outside.

The meadow rippled in its usual serene light. The black woods beyond were motionless, their shadows unbroken by headlights. Only a couple feet from Birdie's window, the walnut tree's sturdy branch waited. Birdie wrestled with the lock and lifted the window in a slow, silent push. A cool, earth-scented breeze passing over her face brought a wave of nausea. Silver light bubbled behind her eyelids. She blinked. The fluttering leaves and rough-barked bough shimmered, gone spectral with vertigo.

If she could just get to her car—

A grinding snarl reverberated through the night air, the sound clawing up the house's walls. Birdie ducked, then peeked out the window.

Crawling from beneath her car, the border collie stared up at her, rising to its paws with its hackles up and bared teeth glinting. As its monotone growl over-rode the whispering leaves, low ripples cut through the grass, and slinking shapes melted out of the dark. The other dogs surrounded the car and sat quietly, and when Birdie backed away from the window, even the border collie settled down, licking its lips.

Birdie pressed a shaking hand to her mouth. Not the tree, then. Maybe she could distract the dogs long enough to get to the car. Was it even unlocked? Where were her keys?

Something rustled next to her. Birdie spun, staring wild-eyed at the gently glowing dollhouses. The mothers, gardening late into the night. The children, standing in the yards past bedtime. The fathers, contemplating whatever-the-fuck indoors, their pale faces stern and wide-awake—

A shadow darted past one of the lit windows.

Birdie's breath stopped.

Mice. The mice had to be back again. That was it.

But the small figure that stalked before a wide bay window was not a rodent. It did not cower. It stood on two legs, stuttered like old Claymation as it walked. It turned its hatted head towards her.

Birdie leapt for the bedroom door, staggering as her legs tangled in the blanket on the rug. In the corners of her eyes, silhouettes flickered, strange intruders sprinting through a God-cursed suburbia. Behind her, something thumped onto the floor.

She was already skidding into the hallway, her shoulder crashing into the antiques outside, sending a dozen or so broken dolls and crumpled bits of house tumbling to the floor. As she clutched her bruising arm, the wall lights flickered madly at the end of the hall, a high electric whine building to a scream. Ozone sizzling—the current shooting down the displays—bulb after bulb flaring with yellow sparks until their filaments *snap-snap-snapped* and delicate glass exploded in chiming showers and a rushing wave of darkness crested over Birdie.

She ran.

Into the tower, slamming into the railing, gazing at the dizzying ground so far below, sprinting in tight circles down the staircase as the dogs barked and howled outside and the flashing lights pursued her. Shadows nipped at her heels. Trembling dolls watched from their houses.

As she wrenched open the door at the bottom of the staircase, the hallway's other doors slammed in sequence. Escape routes, cut off like limbs, a coiling maze of amputations. And Birdie realized—she wasn't being chased.

She was being *led*.

But then she heard her mother crying out, and it didn't matter anymore. Her mother's voice, calling her.

Her mother's voice, a winding and easily broken thread, sobbing her name. Her mother's voice, from the basement.

————

Ten years before, on the night the Daughter ran, she spoke cruelly to her Father over something simple and stupid. A chore he expected of her—to fetch a few boxes from the basement and arrange their contents around the House to his satisfaction. It was still summer, and the Daughter had nowhere to be. The basement was cool and welcoming. The House always made it so. But the Daughter—

The newest Daughter was always so concerned with windows. What birds flitted by. What branches tapped the glass. Whether or not she could unlock them from the inside, whether she could endure the fall without breaking herself. She longed for clouds and shadows. Transient things, heresy against the sturdiness of the Family's House.

So she refused the task her Father set her, snarled down at him from her new adolescent height. Leggy and skittish and ferocious as an unbroken colt. She tried to push past him. Her clumsiness unbalanced her. Her hand slipped from his.

She crashed down the stairs, body cracking against the wood, head splitting against the stones set by her first ancestors, blood spilling over the ancient handiwork of the first Family of the House. Streaming across the mortar. Soaking into the foundations.

And the foundations gasped. And the House breathed.

And where the Daughter, crumpled and crying, saw me not at all, her Father beheld his first angel.

————

"Bridget!" Her mom's voice came through the door, wracked with tears. "Bridget, help me, please."

Birdie crept closer, listening for stairs groaning beneath footfalls. For her father, waiting like a spider in the tunnel of its web. A door slammed somewhere on the second floor, and then another and another. Outside, the dogs howled. Birdie cringed against the wall. But through it all, she didn't hear her father's creaking baritone scolding her mother, snapping out the *Be quiet!* that she'd become accustomed to in early childhood. He wouldn't let her mom make this much noise.

"Is Dad down there with you?" Birdie called.

A dog snuffled along the base of the front door, growling.

"What? Birdie, no," her mother sounded shocked, and a thin wisp of shame rose in Birdie. "No, he's outside. He thinks you're trying to escape. He thinks I'm trying to help you. And I am, sweetie. I am, I just want to help you, I just want to get out of here, and he *knows*."

"You didn't help me." Birdie clenched her fists until her nails dug painful moons into her flesh. "You drugged me."

"He made me do it." She was so distant, as though huddled in the farthest corner of the basement. Birdie laid her ear to the wall until a foul gurgling in the pipes made her pull back. "Birdie, you have to believe me. You do, don't you?"

Birdie's fingertips hesitated on the doorknob.

The chandelier overhead swayed and shuddered. At the door, the dogs whined and yelped. Birdie closed her eyes, watching the play of light and dark on the backs of her eyelids, listening to the dogs and the doors and oh, God, this house would go on forever if it could—

"Birdie," her mother said, and it was the tone she used when she wanted Birdie to hear that it was safe to come out of whatever hiding place she'd found. Tears pattered onto Birdie's shaking fingers. "Birdie. Help me. I need your help."

The doorknob was icy in Birdie's hand.

———

That faraway night, before the scab had set on her wounded skull, the Daughter ran. The woods welcomed her as they welcomed any witch. She cut the love from her heart and the home from her soul, and she wandered in misery for years, which anyone could have predicted.

The Mother had paced from window to staircase, attic to basement, wailing at the loss. But the Father had stayed in the depths of the House, his face shining like a child's at the sight of the House's ghostly heart, gold and flickering as candlelight. Beneath the House's loving gaze, he began his life's greatest work.

Now the Daughter approached that passage again. Now she could correct her terrible choice. Now she could come home. Just as the dogs had trotted in with wagging tails, just as the Mother had held the Father's hand down the stairs. The Father had learned early: they had to enter willingly for the work to take, and to quicken.

The Daughter opened the battered, ancient door, and the House convulsed in joy.

———

A cold, wet wind—a sigh from the mouth of a corpse—swept up from the basement, but Birdie didn't feel it. Birdie had put herself somewhere else.

Lila had warm hands and steady brown eyes. At the first parties—their first dates—Birdie introduced herself like a stranger, not trusting that someone as sparkling as Lila would remember inviting this awkward delivery driver. "I know who you are," Lila said each time, laughing, and each time Lila offered to read her palm, and she always said that the lines stood for something new. Life, love, fate. Love, self, journey. Fate, death, healing. Birdie never believed her, but she let Lila hold her hand for as long as she wanted, angling the silver-blue skin on the hill of her thumb to catch the light. Her black curls never stayed up once she'd had a couple drinks, and they dragged over Birdie's wrist, stinging like sweet jellyfish.

Birdie never believed Lila, but Lila always told the truth. *You're going to buy me a milkshake. I'm going to make you laugh tonight.* On her tiptoes, her giggling lips at Birdie's ear, shivering down her spine. *We're going to go home together.*

For an instant, as the house roared around her, Birdie saw Lila gazing into her eyes, dollar-store disco lights spilling across her now-serious face in a dazzle of fuchsia and blue and gold. *Birdie. This isn't normal.*

"Birdie, please," her mother cried, her voice echoing from a deep, deep place. "Hurry."

Birdie swayed at the threshold. In her worst moments, she thought her mother's relationship with the truth was like watching someone drown in dark water. Truth's head would split the surface, gasping, and then sink again with barely a ripple. Her mother could blink and say that she'd missed it entirely.

When Lila read bliss into her hand, Birdie never believed her, because she never could. Because Birdie knew, in the deepest pit of her stomach, that she saw the truth this way as well.

But as she stared down the shadow-eaten steps, as her mother's pleas echoed up the staircase, as she hesitated, her doom seized the base of her skull, staying her hand on the railing. She knew the truth.

In the basement, her mother and her father were waiting for her.

The Daughter does not descend. Maybe there is no saving her. Or perhaps the Daughter did see me that night. Perhaps she knows. Perhaps that is why, even now, she refuses—oh, but look.

Birdie walked towards her mother's voice. And the House swallowed her whole.

BODY

THE FATHER TURNS THE KEY *in the Mother's forehead, and the Mother swings open, and the Daughter sees but she does not understand.*

The Daughter has never understood.

But afterwards, when shrieks fade beyond echoes, the House arranges the events in a neat and loving scene.

In the basement, broken and unfinished work piles high over the Father's head. Dollhouses—their paint fading, their shutters crooked, their wooden walls splintering with age—await their redemption against the wall. Archived goods crowd the maze of shelves, the upper layers crushing those beneath, threatening a fall. Doll remnants lie scattered across the floor where the Daughter had trembled. They will be cleaned. The work will be done. The Family will build—and build—and build. The dead dollhouse town, freshly repainted, will move to new sunlit rooms, and the dolls will emerge from their tissue-papered graves.

For now, though, the Father has a more urgent task.

The House will remember and cherish the Father's hands as a mother cherishes her infant's miniature fingers. The Father's work, and the Father's care, and the Father's time, so lovingly placed into the fine lines of the scalpel and the steadfast crush of the shears. The Father's blue lips press thin. His stubbled chin trembles, and his skin hangs loose and paper-white beneath strong lights, yet his long, knuckly fingers work with deft, nimble movements to remove organs now unncessary. Time-smoothed flagstones beneath his reddened shoes soak up new blood as it pitter-pats down. He meets the Daughter's emptied eyes—the lids sagging, lividity gathering around the sockets—and he whispers: The world is a wound that won't stop bleeding. But he has staunched the Daughter's injuries. Refurbished her scraped-out emptiness with wood and wires and wallpaper. Laid inside a tiny curled figure, newly sewn with soul. He hopes that she will understand.

The House sighs, and the Father presses a palm to the wall. The House thrums just beyond his warmth.

In the attic, the Mother waits in the mouse-gray shadows among the dollhouses. Her shining eyes stare unseeing, and her hands rest limp on her knees. She is elsewhere in her body. Moonlight falls through the window, and glittering dust hangs within it. Spiders lay out their craft thread by pale thread. The air carries the scent of something burning, miles away, and smoke-perfume seeps into the House without the Mother noticing. A doll watches another doll sleep alone in a bed made for two. The Mother does not notice this either.

Outside, the walnut tree dips its roots in the rich soil; the dogs pace the perimeter of the woods; the long-dead in the graveyard dream. A leaf falls on the hood of the Daughter's car. The Daughter's friend turns over in her faraway bed, restless.

The Daughter sleeps. When she wakes, she will understand.

———

I'm in my childhood bed, sitting bolt upright before I even open my eyes, like one of those novelty baby dolls. *Pull the string and watch her wake!* I'm gasping. I'm clutching a familiar log cabin quilt. Corduroy. Satin. Denim. The things Mom can make from scraps.

Mom. When I glance around, she flashes in the room's darker corners. My mom as religious triptych, illuminated, opening. I suck in a breath. Grind my knuckles into my eyes.

Birds sing outside, and the walnut tree rustles. Beneath the window, the guest-appropriate books and records in my shelves gather dust. Sunlight scatters over the braided rug, spilling onto the cream-colored wingback with the granny-square blanket placed just so, onto the maple secretary desk that's always been too small for me, onto the walls and the dollhouses—

But no sunbeams fall in a broken pattern across the dollhouses, because there's no dollhouses. No shelves. The light stretches smooth over empty floral wallpaper.

I cross the room on unsteady legs—how long was I asleep?—and lay my palm over the faded vines. My pulse spreads over the warm wall, into my fingertips. Were these the renovations Mom kept talking about?

"Mom?"

No answer. The birds keep singing. As I stumble to the door, I realize I'm wearing one of the elaborate pajama sets my parents always got me for my birthday, the kind with button-down shirts and matching slippers and sometimes even a silly hat. I don't get it—I'd sooner sleep naked than wear this. Jesus, was I sick? I must have been, to have such weird dreams, and to sleep through my parents doing what they'd refused to do for my whole childhood: give me a bedroom I didn't have to share with tourists. I duck through the door and freeze.

The houses in the hallway are gone too. The barren space is like bones sucked clean of marrow. Small framed photos hang every few feet: our family walking through the park. Our family in front of the Christmas tree. Our family playing with a grinning border collie. Smiling, laughing, hugging.

We never had a dog. I don't remember taking these pictures.

On the last night, the dogs had howled. Whined outside. I thought they might get in. The house had opened its doors, exploded its lights, chased me from my bedroom into the basement. And in the basement—

"...Mom?" My voice vanishes, eaten by the silence of the house's interior.

I walk faster, careening down the stairs two at a time, calling for Mom again. More bare walls. No little houses with little guys watching. No bored or overenthusiastic tourists.

My dad would never take down this many dollhouses. They're what makes our family a family, according to him. His heritage. I should've known from the second I saw my empty walls.

I veer into the kitchen, muscle memory keeping me dead center on my path, out of the way of any sharp corners or delicate roof details. There's the shining steel sink, the flowers hanging by the window. But no pans on the stove, no dishwasher running. No doll families endlessly sitting down to eat, no painted-smile mothers eternally stirring pots of soup. No dollhouses. No Mom. My breath catches.

The air smells like blood.

Only a trace. A tinge of hot, rotting iron, clotting in my nostrils. It grows stronger, stifling, at the narrow door, the one that opens onto the steep staircase. The one that leads to the basement.

My mother smiling. My mother splitting.

I crack open the door, and the stench floods out. I whimper, crouch, cover my mouth. Beyond the first rickety wooden steps, it's pitch-black. I crawl forward. "Mommy?"

Speaking into the basement has always felt like speaking into the mouth of a monster. My tiny voice gets no reply. But of course it doesn't. I'm alone. It's like something in the house has died. It had been so loud that last night—slamming doors, bursting lights, gurgling inside the walls—and it was almost a relief, learning that things were just as fucked-up as I'd always suspected, that they were wrong on a supernatural scale.

Lila, I want you here. I want you to cradle me close where I kneel against the doorframe, to make me feel small in a way that's safe. I want you, and I don't want to go in the basement. I don't want to find what I've already found.

I wipe my eyes and creep down the stairs. Nine steps to the light cord. I blink into the cave-like darkness, hold the damp railing with both hands. Six steps. My heartbeat surges in my ears until I can hear nothing else. Something hot drips onto my head. Three steps. Under my bare feet, the wood is warm and wet, and I'm weeping as I stretch out from the last step with one hand clutching the railing, the other swiping through the air for the cord, frantic—

I seize it. I pull. The lightbulb buzzes, flickers.

No stone floor soaked with blood. No split-open mother.

No basement.

The single light swings over a black abyss. I'm hanging halfway into oblivion, my straining fingers the only things keeping me from tumbling off the creaking steps that end in midair. I stare down, into the void.

––––––––

Houses shape movement: turn left in the kitchen for the pantry and right for the basement, carry the chairs so they don't scrape the floor, press the key hard into the stubborn lock. On bad days, even years afterward, the Daughter would reach for the wrong drawer in her apartment, grasping for absent spoons.

Habits grow over years, like calluses. When the Daughter brings her friend hot meals at her workplace, her eyes flick from exit to exit. The Daughter goes to bed early without eating much, wakes at midnight, and creeps to her empty kitchen for cereal. She moves in ill-suited silence, half-strangled by her own pulse leaping in her neck, and freezes when she steps on a creaky floorboard. Her ears ring. When she becomes intimate enough with her lovers to fight, her tone goes flat. She excuses herself, sits in the bathroom or the closet, and stares at a single point on the floor.

Good men heal the wounded and fix their dwellings. A bone that's healed wrong must be rebroken. A leprous home must be burned and rebuilt. The Mother and the Daughter now have their own beautiful homes, rooms upon rooms, space upon space, soft beds and the sound of dew falling at dawn. The Father has made this for them, of course. A good Father always provides.

––––––––

Phantom impact of my father's hand against my sternum, *push*. Falling back, stumbling, *crack* against the basement stairs, away from the pit. The light, swinging, wild, a distant and deep-red something shining back through the gloom. Pulsing. Gore under my hands, stairs sticky with it, but I make it back up to the kitchen, finally getting it, finally trying to run. Slamming the door—bloody streaks on the white wall—colliding with the corners, sobbing again when the front door's brass knob sticks solid and the lock clicks back and forth and does jack shit. I step back and kick the door, once, twice, leaving smeared scarlet footprints against the unyielding wood.

Creak. My head snaps up. Someone is walking around upstairs.

"Bridget? Sweetie?" My mom's voice, muffled.

"Mom!" I take the steps two at a time.

She opens my bedroom door, and then I'm in her arms, my head resting on her shoulder, sobbing. She pats my shuddering back. Her familiar floral scent mingles with the raw meat smell. Too soon, she withdraws, frowning at the red mess on her hands. She rubs it between thumb and forefinger.

"Oh, Bridget," she sighs. "You went into the basement, didn't you?"

Fifteen minutes later, I've watched blood swirl pink down the bathtub drain and left smeary red fingerprints on the lavender and cream tiles. I'm clean, warm, dressed in clothes that aren't mine, because the closet only has things that aren't mine. I shift from foot to foot in a tailored sweater and narrow-waisted wool pants, and my mother beams at me from the rocking chair. "You look so grown-up."

I am grown-up. And hot. And itchy. And one of the last things Mom said to me was that she was sorry for hurting me, and now she's smiling like she's kept some kind of promise.

"Why is there blood in the basement?" My voice sounds like I've been hollowed out. My mother sighs and rises from the chair.

"I wanted to be here when you woke up to explain it to you." She licks her finger, cleans an overlooked smudge from near my mouth like it's nothing more than raspberry jam. "You're still such an early riser."

Anger rises acidic in my stomach. "I saw you split in half."

My mother waves her hand like my words are a bad smell and heads to my closet to rummage around the bookshelf against the back wall. I tense as her hand sweeps over the spot where, as a teen, I had hidden all my secrets: vintage smut from estate sales Dad had dragged me to, a fake ID for booze and quick getaways, a burner phone for my girlfriends.

She passes by it. A small *click* sounds. The shelf swings forward, and in the shadows, brass gleams.

A cage? No, a spindly old elevator.

Lila, I'm so tired.

My mother steps inside, loops a ribboned key around her neck, and motions to me. I follow her, a too-tall duckling slouching to fit in the elevator. As it clatters upwards through a narrow shaft of polished wood, my gaze flicks between the filigreed bars and my mother's intact face. "How—"

She shushes me. "You'll see."

The elevator jerks to a halt. Mom slides the brass gate open, unlocks the door behind it with the key at her neck. On the other side, I hear hurried scuffling, like animals scampering into undergrowth. "Hello, boys," she calls.

Boys? I skulk behind her, stuck between a shitty situation I don't understand and another that's possibly even shittier. A dim, empty room greets us, one office chair rotating slowly. My mother strolls out in her cornflower housedress as if this is a trip to the supermarket, and I scramble after her. I hate that I want to grab her sleeve.

Nowhere in our house looks like this, with its ivory domed ceiling and furnishings like a ray-gun gothic office. Around its border, desks and chairs and filing cabinets crowd together, surrounding an organized interior semicircle. On a nearby table, paper piles on the ground in endless folds, nibs scratching ink across it like a polygraph machine. Another wide desk holds a half-dozen old-school monitors scrolling green text. Between the two is a control panel, a clunky array of blinking lights and silver levers with brightly colored knobs, the strangest combination of NASA and Fisher-Price imaginable.

Maybe I *am* imagining it. Maybe I'm dreaming. Or dead. I taste bile and gulp it back down. Lila, I don't want this to be what comes after. Not curtains and locks and ceilings. I wanted an empty road, starry and roofless. I wanted the glowing digits in the dashboard clock to never get too late. I wanted to hear you breathing beside me, even if you were still alive and far away.

I clench my palm to my chest. My heart is beating. I can't be dead if my heart is beating, right?

Beneath my mother's echoing steps, the machines tick and whir, like the parlor's cuckoo clock wall seconds before the bells chime and the tiny mechanized villagers go berserk. And beneath it all, a deep, wet pulse rumbles through the floor.

"What the fuck is happening?" My voice cracks.

My mother touches one of the red levers. "Just remember," she says, "we love you."

She pushes the lever, and—

I mean—I already know, don't I, Lila? I've just been trying not to.

Two oval windows scroll open in the wall beyond the workstation, flooding us with light. Squinting through them, I see myself—a photo, a part of me still thinks, a billboard-sized mirror selfie in front of the bathroom's spotless lavender and cream tiles that I can't remember taking. My hair is combed, pinned flat against my skull. I'm smiling. Each one of my white teeth seems big as a front door. My mother presses a few pleasantly beeping buttons, and the me outside the windows raises her massive hand. She waves.

And I have to understand.

So I do. I sprint for the windows. My eyes. My feet pound the floor of my erstwhile skull, and I vault over the control panel that's replaced my brain. My mother cries out as I scoop up a rusting office chair and raise it high.

How did she think this conversation was going to go?

Mother, kindly let me out.

Nope.

Gracious, Mother, then I suppose I will cope.

Any part of me that would have been all cotton-candy-kindness about this died when I went into that basement, looking for my crying mother, looking for a way out or an ending. I guess now I can be a bitch of a ghost.

I lunge through the dense office labyrinth, crashing into desk corners as I go. The glass looms wide, fish-eye-ing the world outside my dollhouse body into infinity. My once-arms, encased in velvet like a malevolent doll's, seem to extend for miles on either side. The face that isn't mine is frozen in a banal smile, and in the center of my forehead, the small void of a keyhole beckons. I'm laughing as I rear back with the chair, laughing as a part of me gives up, laughing in a wild sob that turns to a shriek of rage as hands close around my waist and arms. Too many hands for just my mother, and far too strong.

I manage to fling the chair. It soars through the air and bounces harmlessly off the inside of my eye.

I'm dragged backwards, my heels scraping the floor, and I kick at the polished shoes that dart into view. I turn my head to scream at their owners, maybe bite off their ears.

A plush mouse wearing a fedora stares back at me, its black button eyes unblinking, and my legs go limp just long enough for the mouse and whatever-the-hell-else is here to wrestle me into the elevator and slam the gate. I huddle on the floor. When my mother's cold fingers touch my knuckles, I withdraw, pressing my back to the far side of the little cage.

"Bridget," she says. Miserable. Like I'm the one mak-ing her miserable. The plush mouse huddles by her side, its felt ears barely reaching her chest, and a faded paper man pats her shoulder with a stained hand. Behind her, light gleams off the molded suit of a plastic man who towers over her. Dolls. Father dolls. With the three of them flanking her, my mother is too realistic. No one would want to play with this sad-eyed thing looking at me through the bars. Maybe that's what Dad thought too.

"Bridget, we did this for you," she says, and the three father dolls around her nod. My actual dad, of course, isn't here.

"Fuck you," I say. My voice is tiny. I am tiny, thumb-sized, easy for my father to flick away. The plastic father doll shuts the door in my face. In the lightless elevator shaft, the jewelry-fine chain clinks, dropping me back down into the haunted house of my own body.

The Father's remade Daughter glides from room to room, heedless of creaking floors. Standing at her fullest height, she seems to float over the guests. The visitors tell her Mother that they look so alike, and the Mother squeezes her Daughter's velvet-covered arm. The Daughter's pink lips draw up in an even smile, and her blue eyes sparkle without ferocity. If the scar on the back of her head twinges, no one winces and whines.

When the guests leave and the dogs wait beneath the quiet House's porch, the Mother and Daughter cook elbow-to-elbow in the kitchen, not flinching as oil pops onto their skin. They fold their aprons and carry dinner trays into the basement, weaving through the shelves, trailing steam among the fragile homes with vacant windows and doors left ajar. The smell of hot bread and salt-savory roast twists with an underlying odor of viscera, an unavoidable putrefaction: blood in the thirsty mortar between the stones. Blood in the old, hungry, sunless soil beneath.

The Family eats at a table where the Father's work forms the centerpiece. Deep shadows pool away from the bright work lamps. Dinner rolls loom like soft hills among half-built houses. The Father chews and swallows, his gaze downcast behind his glasses. The Mother and Daughter chew and spit discreetly into napkins. If the food is delicious or horrible, no one considers it worth mentioning. Conversation is unnecessary when everyone is known so well. The Family dines windowless below the lip of the earth, and the sun sets unseen, as if every glorious hue of every twilight has already been eulogized.

Inside the body, the gnash and crunch of teeth is a flesh-made thunderstorm. The Daughter curls into herself. Outside, the low shriek of knives on porcelain is the only noise. Once the Father has stood, smacked his lips, and resumed work, the Mother and Daughter gather the trays and ascend to the main floor of the House to wash and dry the silver. The Daughter brushes her lips across the Mother's forehead, not noticing the scent of her perfume, and bids her goodnight.

To anyone else—indeed, to her Father—the Daughter is grateful, a forgiven demon. But the House hears her. Her still, small voice screams, a monster devoured by a monster devoured by something even stranger. The first Daughter raised her eyes to a snow-ridden heaven and showed her throat; the newest Daughter crouches and bares her teeth. Where is the covenant after the sacrifice, the long walk down the mountain, the twilight centuries of peace?

The House is meant to think nothing of this. The House thinks nothing of this, save that the Daughter will soon seem at home. She must be at home.

———

I want to lie on the floor, so I'm lying on the floor. I want to die, so I'm not letting myself get up from the floor. What's that article you sent me, the one about people who jump from bridges? That on the way down, they realize everything can be fixed? Dad has the basement hellhole just waiting for me, and I can't tell if he wants me to kill myself or if he's laughing at me because he thinks I can't.

Lila, I'm not going to die. I promise. Or at least, I promise that I won't die any more than I already have. I still have that heartbeat. It's strong. I checked.

The downside of still having a human-ish body: everything swoops around when I move beyond the fetal position, and my teeth keep chattering. It's the stomach-drop of vertigo, but a small part of me keeps chirping that *maybe I'm just hungry!*

That's basically what my mom said years ago after she picked me up off the basement floor. *You'll feel better once you've had some soup and a good night's sleep.* I wish the worst part was that she was right, but that definitely wasn't the worst part.

Besides, of course she was right. Soup always helps. I know you were confused about why I made you so much soup when you were down. Around the third time I brought over a thermos, I remember you saying, "I'm not sick—you know that, right?" And when I'd told you that it was meant as comfort food, you snorted, wound your layers of granny-square blankets up around your chin, and peered up at me with your cheek against my thigh. "My bubbie's honey cake. My nonna's ziti. *That's* comfort food. Not soup."

I didn't mention pastina or matzoh balls in home-made chicken broth. It didn't seem like a good time. Maybe I should have. Maybe I could have told you more about my family like you told me about yours, like how you could still mentally map your way to every one of their apartments, as well as to the best fire escape for a little privacy. Like how you were trying to recreate that map now in our tiny city, even while friends got together and broke up and moved away. We went to goodbye brunches instead of weddings. Perils of a college town.

I have to get back to you.

Before I curled up like a dead spider inside my childhood bedroom—which is now inside my own body, which is inside another, significantly more haunted childhood bedroom—I bruised my shoulder by body-slamming the front door and dented a ladle by smashing it into the kitchen window. Turns out the front door is just a carving, fake down to its glued-on hinges. The kitchen window, fuzzed with blue snow in its cracked corner, is a screen running a ten-second loop of the meadow and trees outside. A flock of starlings resets and resets and resets into the waving grass.

The door to my parents' bedroom is just gone. The trapdoor to the attic is gone. The basement, obviously, is gone. Any door leading outside is either fake or missing. Dad left the hand-painted *Exit!* sign—strawberry runners merrily twining with the cursive letters—hanging in the gift shop over a blank stretch of wall. He did this because he's a sick fuck.

Something thumps and shuffles in my closet, and I scramble towards the door, reaching it right as the lock clicks home. The doorknob rattles uselessly in my hands.

"Now, now."

The voice is stilted and muffled, an old recording just starting to crackle. It sounds like the wet dream of a 1950s propagandist. I just know it's that plastic bastard on the other side of the door.

"Eat my shit and hair," I tell him.

A bit more out-of-sight shambling. "If I had my way, young lady, you'd have no supper. But your mother sent me over with a delicious home-cooked meal—"

"*Fuck* your soup—"

"—and a letter. Make sure you write her back, and don't forget to add the ZIP code."

I say nothing. I'm trembling down to my white-knuckled fists.

"I'm going to unlock the door. Be good, or else." Shuffle of gross plastic feet. Click of the lock. I could lunge forward—I should—but I don't. My mother would say that I know better, but I don't know anything besides the fear that leaves my legs wobbly. I stare at the tender pink of my closet door until the elevator clanks and whirs away.

Once he's gone, I ignore the bright-ribboned goody basket on the floor, instead scratching and scraping at the closet's far wall, trying to find whatever opens it. I don't know what I would do if I got up inside my skull—for now, it's enough that I'm not supposed to be there, so that's where I need to go.

But nothing gives. I snatch up the basket.

Back in my bedroom, sitting on the floor, I read Mom's letter and drink thermos-warmed soup. It's good soup, dense salty broth with thick egg noodles and gold drops of fat floating on the surface, not too much carrot and way too much chicken. It almost makes up for the letter, which is, all things concerned, probably the least terrible thing on my list of Currently Terrible Things.

Dear Bridget—

Well, now you know the renovations we've been doing!

I choke on the chicken noodle, broth shooting up my nose. Droplets spatter my mother's neat purple-pen cursive and stain the creamy museum letterhead.

I know why you're upset. I told your father that you were used to living independently, and this is a big transition. If we talked this out beforehand, it would have been better for you. It certainly was for me. All the space I want for my little hobbies and no more of your father's snoring? Sign me up!

That's why I think it would be helpful for you to see this as a gift, a chance to start over. A place you can really, truly call your own, without any worries about scammy leases and landlords who won't fix your heat even when it's been out for three days in a Boston January (and trust me, I would know about that!).

Except for the dollhouses, which your father removed BY HAND because he loves you, everything is exactly the way it was the day before you set out on your own for the first time. (Well, almost everything. I sewed you all new clothes.) I'm not sure how your father copies everything so perfectly, but suffice to say he's a real "wizard!" Ha ha ha.

You also don't have your computer, and after this morning, I agree with your father about why. Consider yourself grounded for the foreseeable future.

However, you can talk to me (and your father!) anytime by sending us letters, care of the boys upstairs. You can rely on them to be discreet and punctual. When you write your grocery list, add a couple treats for them. And make sure you ask for some cleaning supplies so you can take care of the mess in the front hall.

Stay out of the basement.

We love you so, so much. I'm so happy that we can be together again.

Love,
Mom &

When I flip the paper, I find *DAD* written huge across the back. Maybe the letter was tiny when Mom gave it to him. Maybe itty-bitty things don't embiggen when they leave the dollhouse bodies. I swallow the last of the soup, and it slides hot down my throat.

"Cool," I say. I walk down to the kitchen, rustle through the drawers for the meat tenderizer, and start bashing through the drywall.

———

When the Victorian Daughter drew near her end, she climbed within the House's walls. Her grandnieces fluttered down the stairs in their white nightgowns, drawn by the midnight noise, to find a long rend in the rose wallpaper. A horrific wound of a door, floral scraps in peeled folds, plaster chunks scattered across the floor. Enshrined across the room among ornate dollhouses, the yellowing portrait of their Father's Father's Father saw nothing.

And inside the walls—scratching, groaning, mumbling. The Victorian Daughter in her inconstant state.

The grandnieces called to her through the plaster, their brown eyes red in the shivering candlelight. The Victorian Daughter murmured. One grandniece—a Daughter as well, though she did nothing to deserve the title—peered into the space behind the walls and saw the elderly Daughter embracing—what? Forgotten beams and spiderwebs? Something gold gleamed above her. Something silver gleamed below.

"She still has the axe," the watching grandniece said to the other, who withdrew her ear from the wallpaper with a gasp.

They sat on the low sofa together as though courted by the morning's early hours, serenaded by the Victorian Daughter's low and loving litany that neither of them could understand. Their brother was at school. Their parents were already in the family cemetery.

In the morning, they begged a neighbor to pry the Victorian Daughter free, and afterwards, the grandniece who had investigated the wall the night before stepped into the cramped passage. She found fingernail scratches where the Victorian Daughter had resisted removal, but nothing that glittered. Nothing to explain the two shining reflections over the Victorian's Daughter's head, like yellow coins in the dark. The eyes.

The grandnieces were horrible children. They ran before grass grew on the Victorian Daughter's grave, threw themselves into the arms of strangers, and never returned to the ever-adoring House. They did not understand what drew the Victorian Daughter into the walls: that she did not seek to flee from a tragedy, but to escape into the only arms that would love her as she needed to be loved.

How could they not recognize it? When the first grandniece looked upon the Victorian Daughter laying her wilted brow upon the body—the memory—of the House? And when the second grandniece, her ear to the wall, heard the whispers of not one voice, but two? I know not the palm that holds you over the flames, only my hand reaching for yours. But you cannot carry me. *How could they not comprehend it?*

It mattered not. The memory of the Victorian Daughter faded. The spirit of love was left to rattle in the walls, heard only by a few, its wailing mostly attributed to dolls unhappy with their wooden lives. The newest Father heard it, and spoke gently to its miniature incarnations. The newest Daughter heard in her Father's voice all the tenderness she never earned.

As the newest Daughter—the last Daughter—rends her own walls, what love does she have? What love does she even deserve?

————

Dust clouds around me as the meat tenderizer shreds the drywall. Chips shotgun past my ears, ping off my forehead. Strips of wallpaper and rubble hang like cuticles. My grunts turn to coughs in the plaster-smelling fog, but it can't be long now. Almost through. My father made sure I knew this house from ceiling to cellar, so I know where the brick meets the wooden additions of the Victorian era, and I know it's a clusterfuck. Fragile to start with, and poorly maintained for decades afterwards.

A desperate optimism (and also the dust) seizes the breath in my lungs. Lila, you say I'm the most hopeful nihilist you've ever met. When I see you again, I'll tell you it's because I can recognize when things are shit, but I know that they can't be shit everywhere. I'll say, "I've cleaned out the top dresser drawer, if you still want it." I'll ask, "If we had a dog, what would we name it?" I'll tell you that I'm not ready yet, but that I'm tired of waiting until I'm ready.

I haul back again and again, the impact of metal on wood vibrating up my arm into my gritted teeth. With every blow, the meat tenderizer deforms a bit more. It punches through the moldy ass-end of the Victorian facade—not nearly as pretty on the inside, is it?—and sends splinters flying like fireworks. Bash. Bash. Bash.

Crunch.

The whole thing sticks in the wall, and my sweaty palm slips off the handle. I breathe hard and hack up cloudy gray spit. There better not be asbestos in my dollhouse body. I try to yank the tenderizer out, and it shrieks against the wood in a way that sets my teeth on edge before it pulls free with a sound that could be described as *splorp.*

You could also describe it as wet, horrible, and deeply goddamn troubling.

I stare at the tenderizer. The head is drenched red and stinks like fried iron. Something trickles, drip-drip-dripping down from the hole in the wall.

More than a hole—a wound. A perfect little pocket of flesh opening into the used-to-be-me outside the dollhouse, a pinhole sore gurgling blood in oozing, pumping bursts. It dribbles over broken wood, pools on dust-covered floors, stains pale oak boards. Beside me, the window clicks over to a loop of an orange sunset. Clots float atop the gilded blood pond like autumn leaves. How romantic.

You told me once you work best when you're angriest, that sometimes you think about climate change or Karens when you need to get shit done. You told me sometimes you came over afterwards, all sweaty, and put your head on my lap just to calm down. I stroked your damp hair, pushed tickling ends away from your nose. You said it helped. I missed the point and told you I couldn't imagine getting anything done when I was that angry.

Babe, forgive me. I love your chin against my thigh. And I didn't know my own rage.

I white-knuckle my tenderizer, crunching boards into the meat and ripping at them with my free hand, peeling them away to reveal the slow-beating crimson mass beyond. The wall gleams and stinks. Slick blood pours hot over my hands, runs rivers up my wrists and arms. It tides over my feet and soaks into my socks. When I bury the tenderizer into flexing, banded muscle, a vein geysers into my face. I splutter, mouth gone sticky with the metallic tang of my own meat.

Something thunks at my feet as I unstick the tool: its dented metal head, barely visible beneath the carmine gush now filling the living room. I bury my hand in the tumbling blood. My fingers sink into flesh and nothing happens. I brace my legs and push. No change. No daylight. Nothing. I shove so hard that I slip and splash into the gory pond beneath me. Thick crimson sludge swirls past in a warm and reeking river, carrying splinters of wood and plaster. Vertigo swoops through my stomach again.

I stumble-slosh over to the couch, gripping fabric that's already soaking up the lapping red wavelets. The window switches to blue moonlight and cricket sounds. The lights flick off. Past my feet, the blood now flows black and shining.

What did I expect? I pop out like the product of a wandering womb and immediately fall to my death? I wriggle free from between my own ribs and get nabbed by "the boys upstairs" about three seconds later? I spend a few days scurrying around my family's giant-ass house like an escaped hamster before I get eaten by a dog, as befits a hamster with dreams above its station?

I wish I could ask you what to do. If I could talk to you, I'd tell you that I never want to say goodbye again.

But on the way down from the bridge, I guess everything is obvious.

I don't know how much time passes—I must have watched a wispy little cloud kiss the moon's cheek a million times in that dumb window, looping to eternity—but eventually I get up and stuff a few afghans from the couch into the wall-wound. Hopefully that'll be enough to keep me from waking up to a blood-drenched everything.

Wouldn't be the first time. Heyo.

Upstairs, I barricade my closet door while the cricket soundtrack fades and starts again. In the bathroom mirror with its etched-flower border, I am a dripping horror, lank and red and cadaver-eyed. It would be cool, but, you know. I sit in the shower until the water goes from red to pink to clear for the second time today. The hot water runs out while I'm scrubbing scabby clumps from behind my ears.

When I finally go to bed, exhausted but wide awake, I stare up at the tiny glow-in-the-dark stars I painted with my first girlfriend. She was convinced Dad wouldn't be able to notice them, and she was right about that, although he did notice her face flinching away from mine when he came into the room. He screamed at us until she left. I didn't stick up for her. She broke up with me. I kept my girlfriends a secret after that: no visits inside the house, no phone calls except for the burner, no emails and no MySpace shenanigans.

Did I ever tell you this?

The stars are beautiful, glowing their soft green. Ellie had good ideas. At some point after I ran away, Mom repainted the ceiling, and when I came back five years ago, there was just a void over my bed. It's nice to have them again. I blink, the stars winking into the soft shadow of almost-asleep.

When Mom said that Dad had made the house exactly the way it was when I left home, I thought it was a lie. So many missing rooms, and, of course, the most important thing from that night is gone. The thing that happened in the basement. But some of what's been lost from back then really is here.

My eyes fly open. Oh, shit.

I toss back the covers, drag the dresser away from the closet, and wriggle inside. At the back of the pitch-black room, I pray I'm the only one in here and choke back a scream when an empty coat sleeve trails over my wrist.

I feel along the underside of a bookshelf until my fingertips skate over thick, crinkly paper. I bite down on the inside of my cheek to keep from giggling as I pull the manila envelope free.

Careful, careful. Big envelope clutched to my chest, I squeeze back out of the closet and replace the dresser. Only then do I dump the package's contents onto my bed.

There, among the scattered '70s Playboys, lying next to a fake ID and a few pills that do God-only-knows-what, is my old black burner phone.

———

I should destroy her.

The House. The House should destroy her. If the Daughter understood for the barest second—if she remembered the smallest glimpse of what the House remembered—oh, she'd turn to embers from the inside out. She would burn herself down.

How many times has it been said within these walls. Ungrateful Children. All the meat their Fathers have sacrificed—all the silence their Mothers have endured—all so that the Children could frolic like fools adorned with blooms. A fresh garland around their head, a bright chain around their neck. May there be biting insects in the verdant crown, may there be harsh metals in the chain, may there be a reckoning upon the Child who forsakes the Family.

How many times has it been said. The House grows weary with it. The House sees the flower stems woven into new stems and the links of the chain joined into new links, and the House's memory wanders.

A bitter dawn. Fingertips carved from painful ice. Three centuries ago, the first Daughter checked the traps at the wintry forest's edge and spotted gleaming eyes. In the snare, a small white hunting dog shivered, its scarred muzzle freshly bloodied, its gnawed leg steaming in the snow. The first Daughter watched it lift its lips over its teeth and snarl. The first Daughter blew warm air into her cupped hands. The first Daughter carried a club. Her Family's soup had thinned in recent days.

The dog snapped at the Daughter's hand. She'd reached out to comfort it, cooing, promising a quick end, but the dog writhed and screamed at the end of the snare. Its eyes flared wild with pain, but remained steadfast on hers. Refusing.

The Daughter set her jaw and lunged again for the dog. Hot agony crushed through her palm as teeth punctured frozen skin and scraped bone. The Daughter's gasp rose as mist, but she wrapped her rent hand around the dog's blood-stubbled snout, holding it in place. With her other hand, she loosened the snare.

The dog fled, leaving a red trail in the snow, and the Daughter slumped back against a tree. Her injury shook, dripping a deep crimson well at her feet. How foolish, she thought, looking into the snowy woods where the dog had disappeared. How utterly foolish she'd just been, with her Mother's cheeks hollowing and her Brother's eyes sinking and her Father's brimstone voice going hoarse. How foolish. She smiled.

Later, in the watered-milk light of early morning, her Father saw her wrapped hand bleeding through its makeshift bandage. She said she'd fallen while checking the snares. A pause. Her Family, frozen at the sound of her lie.

How many times has it been said: there's always a Daughter in the worst of times, until there isn't. There's always a Daughter, destroyed. The House remembers.

———

The burner phone's tiny screen glows with pixelated snowflakes. This is it—a way out. Or, if not *exactly* an exit, not a door or a window, it's at least a keyhole I can yell through. I'm two-thirds of the way through *9-1-1* when my thinking brain catches up with whatever the rest of my mind is doing. My finger hovers over the scuffed *1*. I call them, and then what? Cops show up, nod at the front door like they did last time, and then leave again? And then my parents know that I have something that can contact the outside world? Yeah, great.

Or! I could call them and make a bomb threat. Then, I somehow hijack my skull while the police are heading over. I use the ensuing chaos to run away. Except I have no clue how to drive the dollhouse body, and I probably wouldn't get very far even if I did, because fleeing the scene of a bomb threat is a bad look.

Or, maybe I call them and say that there's a fire, and I hijack my skull (still don't know how I'd do that), and I *actually* start a fire to create even more chaos, and then I burn to death because, again, I don't know how to pilot a big lesbian mecha.

See? You're dating a smart cookie, Lila. At least I know that I'm fucked.

The phone screen burns blue in the gloom, and I feel like I'm seventeen, and it's just too much. It's too much to be in this house again.

So I punch in your number—yeah, I memorized it, of course I memorized it—and with each digital *beep*, my heart accelerates. My hands shake as I raise the flip phone to my ear. The connection grinds, clicks. I gnaw my already-too-short thumbnail.

I tell myself that I won't cry this time. I'm gonna be cool for you, you know? I'm not going to talk, or breathe weird, or freak you out. I'll hear your voicemail message, or your real voice, and you'll think I'm a glitchy, silent robocall, and—I'll get a chance to wish you goodbye.

The phone rings.

Once. Twice. And then:

"Hello?" Your voice is groggy, and I can see you. Your black hair curlier than usual, flat on one side, your cheek a deep peach where it's been pressed into your pillow. A line of drool streaked past the double moles on your chin. If I were there, you'd smell warm and sweet, like tea with too much honey. My breathing stutters, a storm-cloud sob gathering in my throat, and you—

"*Birdie*?" All traces of sleep vanish. Your voice is raw. "Birdie, is that you?

I can't, I can't pretend not to be here. I swallow twice before I can speak. "Lila."

"Are you okay? Where are you?"

"I—I'm still at my parents'."

"What? Bird, it's been days! You haven't answered my texts, you haven't picked up my calls—what the fuck is going on? Are you safe?"

"I'm fine." I sound like a wounded duck.

"You suck at lying. Tell me what's going on."

I close my eyes. On the backs of my eyelids, I watch my girlfriends, shadowy in the front seats of their cars. Crossing their arms, leaning their heads against steamed-up windows, set jaws silhouetted by fireflies. Sick of sneaking out to me every summer night. *They won't believe you.* I sink onto the floor beside the bed, draw my knees up to my chin.

"Birdie." Your tone crackles with desperation.

"I'm not safe," I say. You're not going to believe me, but I still have to play this out. "I can't get out of the house."

You swear. You hardly ever swear, and you've done it twice so far. "I'm calling the cops."

"Don't!" I grip the phone, pitch my voice back to a whisper. "They won't help."

The one time I'd called before—trying to stay awake, blood clotting in my hair—they sent an officer who chatted with my father at the front door, waved to me at the top of the stairs, and left. My dad had assured him the whole thing was a misunderstanding. That I was just causing trouble. As the officer drove off, Dad looked at me the way he looked at spiders in the dollhouses. I want to tell you this—I'm *going* to tell you this—but I hear drawers clunking open and realize what you're doing.

"I'm coming to get you," you say.

"You can't do that either." The dogs. My parents. My own body. "It's dangerous."

"I'm sorry, Bird, but then why did you call me? Did you just wanna say, 'Hello, I'm kidnapped, guess we won't be seeing much of each other anymore?'" Your keys jingle.

"It's not that simple!"

"Why, because your parents can't know we're dating?" You snort, but your voice is straining high and wild. "Because they've put a cute little sign outside that says *Absolutely No Gays, Thanks*? Because they've locked you in, like, a literal tower?"

"No, because—"

"Because you're actually in a secret sub-basement filled with haunted dolls? Where are you calling me from? Did you steal a tourist's phone?"

"This isn't funny—"

"No, it isn't." A car door slams. "You didn't answer my calls, and you didn't show up for work, and nobody had heard from you, and your car wasn't back, and I thought you were *dead*. I already called the cops once, by the way, so yeah, I guess you're right, they're full of crap. But as far as I can tell, you're not dead, and you need help. So what isn't simple about this?"

"My dad used evil magic to turn my body into a dollhouse." I cover my soaking saltwater face with my free hand, my tone yodeling into a total breakdown wail. "And I'm locked *inside* it. And it's being driven around by other *dolls*. And I'm, like, *three inches tall*."

Silence. Silence so loud it could fry my eardrums. When you take a shaking breath, I think I might crack in half. Again. "Okay," you say. There's a couple deep inhales, a sniffle, a cleared throat. "So, when we go out on dates now, you can wear heels without making me look like a hobbit?"

"Fucking—just hang up on me." I grind my palm into my streaming eye. Of course you don't believe me. Which is fine, by the way. Probably for the best. "Just tell me I'm an asshole. You don't have to drag this out. I'm crazy. You've finally realized this relationship is a bad idea. Just go back to bed. Please."

"I'm not sleeping after that, Bird." You've gone quieter. Christ, you're still planning on coming out here.

"I just wanted—" I try to think it through. How to make you stay. What lies I can tell to make you go *Wow, that's officially Too Much*. But my brain ticks like a slow clock, and I'm terrible at lying. "I just wanted to tell you that I love you, and I want you to be safe."

"Uh-huh. Love you too. What's your parents' address?"

"And I never want to say goodbye to you again." My throat thickens. "But I think—"

"Birdie, look. Either you're telling me the truth, in which case I need to come help you, or you're having a full psychotic episode in your abusive childhood home, in which case I still need to come help you." Your voice gets more distant from the speaker, and a soft *shushing* comes through. You must be ponytailing your curly hair, catching the flyaways in a half dozen bobby pins, your final sign of serious shit starting.

You continue: "At this point, I do not care if you break up with me. If you tell me that you hate me, that my breath stinks, that my taste in Halloween costumes is terrible and that you'd prefer to be locked in your parents' creeptastic dollhouse rather than move in with me—I still don't care. I'm coming to get you. So tell me how to help. Otherwise, I'm just going to ram the front door and go from there."

Tears cascade down my face. On your end, a car engine coughs, struggling to turn over. You mutter, "Come on, you bastard."

"I wanna move in with you," I say. My throaty sobs kind of ruin the admission—sorry that I can't be cool for you—but you understand, and you go quiet. I tilt my head back. The stars overhead are holding onto their faint glow. "Lila, I wanna live with you."

A staticky, shuddery breath comes through the phone. You sniffle. "Well, maybe—maybe if your parents like me, we'll be tossed in the dollhouse attic together, huh?"

My soaked eyelashes stick to my cheeks as I laugh with you. Panic burbles out of me. "Lila, oh my God, don't die. Please don't die."

"Never," you say. The engine finally growls to life. "Now tell me where I need to be."

I tell you to wait in the woods outside the meadow, to not text my cell number, to not call me on this one. I tell you not to pet any dogs. I tell you that I'll have a better plan soon, and that I'll call you when I can. I tell you that the house is fucking haunted.

I tell you the second-most important thing: do not ever come inside the house.

I tell you the most important thing: I love you.

When I hang up, I look at the grainy phone screen, and a pit opens inside me. The battery's on its last pip. I kept the burner phone's cable in my backpack so I could charge it at school. And on the night that I ran away—I squeeze my eyes shut, praying to remember something different—my backpack was too bloody to take with me, so I left it behind.

In the basement. Which is gone.

Shit.

———

How strange it is to wake from dreams convinced that one's empty hands should be full. The House no longer dreams, but it does see the troubled faces of its Family, their half-asleep anguish as they sit up in their blanket-tossed beds, sweat gleaming. They look into the dark and do not suspect the House of looking back. Their faces are honest.

The first Son—the second Father—rose often like that over the course of his long years. His nightmares wore early wrinkles into his brow and mouth. He startled at the smallest sounds: twigs at the window, mice in the cellar. He went down to the basement, always to the basement, and stood in the middle of the cold stones, staring into corners where his candlelight barely touched. He hoped for the flame to flicker, to be snuffed out. He hoped to feel the presence of something more than the shadows before him: his sister's fingers closing over his wrist and pulling him along into a part of the House that he hadn't known existed. The unknown cellar below the cellar where she'd waited for him.

Nothing ever happened, though the House was always awake with the Son.

But something had befallen them. In their first winter in the house, when the soup had weakened nearly to water, the Son fell into a feverish stupor from which he could recall nothing: nothing, that is, except for his sister's cool hand against his. And when he woke with the feeling of her phantom fingers in his palm—where had she gone?

The House itself had woken only once. Only once, and all at once, as if countless eyes stared transfixed and trembling. Its skin stretched drum-tight, veins snapping and spilling, pooling bruise-purple at the floor. Its legs, folded on themselves and themselves and themselves, shrieking beneath scrabbling twists of arms. The House awoke crushed between the walls and the ghost-void behind the walls, and the House was the walls and the roof and the ashes choking the stones. The House's scratching hands were splinters in a cobwebbed rafter, and the House's screaming mouth was the dust in a forgotten corner, and no one heard the House because there was nothing to hear. Fingers in the doorframe, eye in the windowpane, foot in the coals, teeth in the tallow floating in the wax, and no one saw because there was nothing to see.

Carved meat and cut bones and melted fat in the bubbling pot. That was all they saw. The House woke to the smell of smoky meat and thick stew and the sight of a wooden spoon in the Son's sleeping mouth, and the House has never slept since.

Nothing happened in the basement when the Son sought his sister. But once upon a time, something had, something his parents brought with them to their final bed beneath the meadow grass. What was it?

"What was it" is the wrong question. As the last Daughter moves blind within her body, as she swears her love undying, as she refuses to sleep, it's more correct to ask this: "Why hasn't it stopped?"

———

Neither of us are great at plans. If we were in charge of putting on a party, then you'd welcome people in through the front door, and I'd shoo them out the back.

Quick, leave, this is a disaster, we only have old celery sticks and cheap wine!

You trust everything will work out, because didn't it always when you were growing up? Your family whirled around each other in cramped kitchens like dozens of perfect dancers. That's why you keep making flyers, making time, making space for all those get-togethers: no-buy swaps, high teas, crafternoons, open-mic karaoke nights in the open air of the city park. Eventually, it'll be perfect.

Meanwhile, I overthink into full overwhelm, and at that point, it's easier to just abandon everything. But something's changing, isn't it? You're coming to get me now, and I have to get serious, Li.

I power off the phone to save battery. I pace circles around my lightless bedroom, listening for noise at the closet door. The "boys" upstairs are the biggest obstacle, them and Baby's First Evil Lair controlling my body. Do I distract them? "Disable" them?

I creep downstairs for coffee. The blood from the wall-wound has spread in a thin scabby slush from the parlor all the way to the kitchen. It stinks like a massacre, and when I open the fridge, the congealing gunk shivers like half-set cherry Jell-O. I make coffee while blood marinates the bottom of my pajama pants. I do it like it's normal, like I'm not about to hurl. Lila, I've basically busted a water line stuffed with gore. If that hasn't gotten the dolls to come down from my skull, then what will?

I plunk myself at the kitchen table. The coffee tastes meaty—unlucky, how smell overrides flavor—and next to me the window displays a nighttime scene of the meadow with a dog watching the house. No wind in the trees. No video at all in this one. I guess I'm supposed to be sleeping, so Dad didn't bother.

You can tell a lot about the way you're expected to act based on how a space is set up. In the house—the real one, not this crap—all the dolls are glued down, so you know they're not toys. And here, the front door is just a bit of molding with a doorknob that doesn't even turn. My parents are saying I shouldn't even be thinking about going outside. I guess they don't think I have any business down in the basement either. Took them long enough to figure that one out.

The light above the basement-stairs-to-nowhere is still on, by the way. I haven't gone back to turn it off, and I don't plan to, not after what I saw. Or didn't see. I don't know. Now that it's night, the cracks around the door glow. Not yellow, though. Bright, haloed scarlet, like a flashlight held against a finger. I sip my coffee, watching as the light trembles—something's made the bulb shake—and I decide I've had enough coffee. I try to ignore the door's reflection in the kitchen window as I rinse out the half-empty mug (because that's what you do with dirty dishes). A *plip-plip* from the parlor mingles with the cricket noise, but I hear nothing from the basement void.

With the carpet squelching under my feet, I go back upstairs. I'm not really more awake. It just feels like a mother dog is carrying me around by the back of my neck. I rub my eyes.

I'm supposed to be asleep, to be wearing the clothes Mom sewed for me, to be making nice with the father dolls who can barge into my room through my closet at any time. I'm supposed to—my eyes fall on Mom's letter, trodden on in the middle of the carpet—I'm supposed to be a good daughter.

And Lila, I get it. I totally know why the father dolls haven't come down about the blood.

I check my top desk drawer, squinting in the dim light. Museum stationery, personalized with my full name, gleams white as smiling teeth next to a collection of fountain pens. It's the only shit in there, which means that I'm right about what I need to do.

Well, if Mom wants to talk, we can talk. I can give them sorries and shame. I can give them a whole grovel-tastic apology, lying through my broken doll mouth.

Mom used to tell me, "Well, it's like your father says: if you don't have your family, you have nothing." And I was so confused by that, because, like, Dad never said that to me? I never heard him say it, anyway.

I got it eventually, though. For Dad, it wasn't a "universal truth," one of those pattery sayings you can get on a coffee mug. No. For Dad, it was aspirational. And they want to give me something to aspire to.

If I was still doing things my old way, I'd hesitate instead of flicking the cap off a fancy pen, losing it in the dark. I'd freak out about what to do once I actually got to the skull. How would I take control from the dolls, and what would I do about my parents? How would I time everything to make sure that you were waiting outside? How was I going to deal with the dogs? Did I even know how to drive this thing?

I guess I'm still freaking out about it. But I'm trying to learn from your parties. Trust what I do know. And Lila, I'll tell you this: if I know one thing, it's how to act normal in shitty circumstances.

The plan might not be perfect. But if it gets me back to you, then that's close enough.

———

The imperfect House has been caught in its own memories.

It returns to itself, alighting onto beams and floorboards and spider nests. Lights burn too bright. Doors slam too easily. The last Mother flinches in the glare, glancing around (but this isn't new—she was afraid when she came here). The last Father presses his ear to the cold floor, his glasses jostling on his skull. He had always been attentive, eager to learn even the furious tilt of his Father's chin. He'd mastered it when he was still a round-faced child.

"What's going on?" he asks now. "Beloved, tell me."

With that, the House quiets, soothes the frenetic thump-thump-thump *of overlapping hearts behind the wallpaper, beneath the stones. A good House is a quiet house.*

The last Daughter glides down the stairs, her coltish gait replaced with parade-quality sophistication. The dolls inside her skull guide her forward, their hands flying over dials and levers to produce a harmonious imposter. The mouse doll chitters his tiny teeth and taps several buttons to raise the Daughter's pale hand. Between her stolen fingers is a minuscule envelope. The Father plucks it free. The House looms over all of them, occupying the table, the magnifying glass, the lamp swinging from its cord. The Father splits the envelope and reads the looping script. He sighs, half-smiles.

"Mother will be relieved." With that, he passes back the note. "Bring it to her. We'll speak to Bridget tomorrow evening."

The dolls swivel the last Daughter's body around and guide it up the stairs, towards the kitchen where the Mother scrubs pots for the dishes she doesn't eat. In the basement, the Father's gaze travels over the empty air. "You're here, aren't you? Keeping me company."

The House is always here.

"Is there anything I need to know about her? Anything else she's planning?"

The overhead light blinks once. Twice. The Father's glasses glint over his bright eyes. He turns back to his projects, takes up a fine brush dipped in black. Under the sharp odor of paint, sweet rot persists. "Good. That's one less thing to worry about."

When the last Daughter came home as an infant, the Father had held her to his chest, their synchronous breathing a soothing, tidal sound. And when the last Daughter fled from her home for the first time, she'd bled from a wound the Father had inflicted.

Oh, God. What's the purpose of remembering everything with equal weight, as though each moment were a blade of grass in a field? As though some memories are not a different type of existence? No, it isn't only grass. Saplings are meant to grow there, and wildflowers, and moss in the quiet places. The dead sleep—do they sleep?— in the wormy ground beneath their stones. The House has made terrible mistakes. But the meadow could grow. The forest could make its slow march across the open land. And the House could change, too.

———

In what passes for morning in my dollhouse body—I have no idea if it's actually morning, because why would the windows need to reflect what's going on outside?—I make oatmeal and coffee, and I vomit in the sink. The gore stench feels like two hands taking my skull between them and squeezing until only bloody perfume is left.

I push my hair back, expecting the scar on the back of my skull that you found once and that I refused to talk about, but my fingers skate over smooth skin. No scar. Shock jolts through me, but only for a second. Of course the scar is gone. Why wouldn't my father erase it? My stomach roils again as I stir the gloopy oatmeal.

Blood's soaked all the way up into the second floor, staining the wallpaper. I touched it on the way down-stairs, and the sticky plaster was weak under my hand. I keep forgetting this place is tiny. But the blood knows. It understands what size everything actually is when it moves through the dollhouse like spilled tea through a towel.

On the first floor, a puce scab has crusted over, springy beneath my slippered feet (I'll ask before I ac-tually tell you this gross shit in person, Li, don't worry). Birdsong chitters from the cracked window in the kitch-en. Even halfway to static, the misty morning scene is so fresh it aches, promising dewy air that would wash out the blood's stinking miasma. No windows open in the dollhouse, obviously. Mom probably gets to air out her body when the rooms get too stale, but I'm not allowed to open myself up.

"Shameful." The crackling word comes from over my shoulder.

I whirl around, one hand halfway to the knife block before I realize that it's the Plastic Father. He hunches, his molded-on fedora scraping the ceiling, his shoulders curled as though ready to pounce. Too big a doll in too small a house. His eyes fix on me, two lumpy-painted blue dots around black pinpricks. I inch closer to the knives. Doubt I'd be able to actually stab him, though—his suit is a glinting, gummy carapace. The blade would bounce off. Christ, he's huge.

"A young lady like you should know how to keep house," he says. His melty-looking plastic smile doesn't open when he talks, but his voice booms out like sound from a TV. "What will the boys think?"

"They can—" *Think whatever they fucking want*, I almost say, and then bite my tongue. "You're right, I'm sorry."

His matte gaze doesn't waver from my face. If I try to leave, will he grab me? Am I allowed to move? A wisp of smoke from the overcooking oatmeal cuts through the blood.

"Won't you offer me a cup of that fine coffee?"

I don't want to turn my back to him. I pour a mug with my shoulders pointed sideways, glancing at him the whole time. His arms hang at his sides, overly articulated fingers twitching along each of their four joints. Against the pockmarked flesh of the floor, his shiny shoes are lifeless plastic slabs. Heavy enough to kick my toothpick-thin ribs into splinters. He shifts, and the coffeepot trembles in my hand.

"A good hostess asks if their guest wants cream or sugar."

I grit my teeth. "Do you want cream or sugar?"

He nods once, hat brim squeaking against the ceiling.

I have to look away to see into the refrigerator. Over the yellow-lit fridge door, beady black eyes flash. I stumble backwards—"Fuck!"—and collide with cold plastic.

Plastic Father lays a massive hand on my shoulder. I flinch away.

"Language," he says. His recorded voice grinds into a low growl. I cower against the fridge, head whipping between Plastic Father towering over me and Mouse Father scratching a paw at his embroidered nose. His eyes are bright, empty buttons sewn into worn gray velvet, but when he raises its snout and sniffs at me, his teeth are too sharp, too yellow, to be from a toy.

The knives are too far away now. If I kick the Plastic Father between the legs—but he's a doll. I can't count on any vulnerable bits. My breath wheezes, lungs filling with the scent of blood that's no longer mine. The room tips.

And Plastic Father takes two strides backwards, jointed legs clicking, shoes crushing rancid liquid from the scab. His skin-tone smile somehow widens.

"What a lovely surprise! Mr. Mouse has joined our party. How about you give him a jolt of that delicious java?"

Lila, you don't actually *need* to hurt someone, as long as they know that you *can* hurt them. I struggle to my feet and pour another cup of coffee, drops splattering the counter and scalding my hand.

"Cream or sugar?" I manage. The Mouse Father wears a tiny bow tie, a felt hat.

He shrieks.

"Life isn't sweet enough for him," the Plastic Father translates, his radio tones ricocheting off the walls. His body covers the whole doorway. "Sugar, please."

I stir the coffees. The spoon clinks against porcelain, but not loud enough to cover my shaky breathing. Plastic Father's hand engulfs the mug when I pass it to him. I hold out the other cup as far as I can from my body. Mouse Father's pink nose twitches. He darts forward, snatching the drink from my fingers in a flash of little claws, and buries his snout in the steaming mug, lapping and gurgling. I recoil.

"Mm-mm, that is good coffee." Plastic Father lowers the mug, revealing a line of moisture over his closed mouth. "You'll make some lucky man a fine wife."

He stares at me, and I know that he knows. I shuffle over in front of the knife block again. "So are you just dropping by, or...?"

"All business, are we? Well! Mr. Mouse, won't you oblige her?"

The mouse shuffles forward, scrabbling inside his gold-buttoned vest and producing an envelope with my mother's handwriting. I take it. The top has already been ripped open, and I try (and fail) not to grimace. Plastic Father's ever-widening smile broadens again, stretching his face with a creak.

"Your parents remind you to stay out of the basement, and say that they would be delighted to have a pleasant chat with you tomorrow evening at five. Care to pass on an RSVP?"

Another warning to stay out of the basement. They really think I'm going to kill myself. I fold the letter and tuck it in my back pocket. "Tomorrow afternoon would be *grand*."

"Exquisite. We'll come down to collect you. Look your best, and brush up on your manners. It's a terrible time for a faux pas." Plastic Father raises his cup to his lips once more, letting out an exaggerated *Aaaah*. "We'd best hit that dusty trail, Mr. Mouse."

Mouse Father's mug bounces off the scabby floor with a dull thunk, and I jump. The plush creature squeaks again, a pained series of *eek-eek-eek*s, while he stumbles forward on his hind paws. Plastic Father holds out his massive arms as though to a toddler just learning to walk. "There you are. Very good."

The mouse scrabbles to hold on to the edge of his rubbery suit jacket. This time, I manage to keep my face expressionless.

Plastic Father straightens. "Thank you again for the coffee, Miss Goodbain."

He tips his cup over the sink, and the entire serving swirls down the drain, leaving behind only a wisp of steam. I ball my hands into fists. At the sight, Plastic Father's sealed-together smile is the biggest it's ever been. "We anticipate this is the start of a wonderful neighborly relationship. Come along, Mr. Mouse."

He pivots and hulks out the door, practically folding himself in half to wriggle through, but the entire time, he keeps one hand on the back of the Mouse Father. Supporting him. Guiding him. I slide a butcher's knife from the block. I imagine throwing it, pinning Plastic Father's hand to Mouse Father's back.

But we both know I haven't gotten that impulsive— not yet—so instead I watch Mouse Father's pink corduroy tail drag heavy along the floor and vanish from sight. As Plastic Father's footsteps fade out, I kick aside the mug that Mouse Father dropped, jam the cool steel blade home in the knife block, and get to work on making more coffee.

The smoking oatmeal is beyond saving. I've lost my appetite anyway.

———

The House brings its many eyes to the attic. It watches the summer woods. The luna moth undersides of the deep green leaves flutter and flash in the slightest breeze, and below them, tourists come and go, invisible until they reach the meadow's edge. In that long-ago summer, the first Daughter and her family had watched the trees as well, certain someone would come for them. "They'll soon realize their folly," the Father said. "They have need of me."

The Mother watched for her friends. The Son watched for a puppy that he'd left behind. The Daughter dreamed that something stranger would come from the trees—a flying ship with pearly sails, a carriage drawn by unicorns, an angel of the Lord with a gentle face—and abscond with her to somewhere wilder and more distant still.

But nights grew longer. The leaves changed hue as though eaten by an unseen and deathly flame. And once the first snow fell, only the Father still held faith that any day now, any day now, the woods would deliver someone to them. Ice made his mind brittle and ferocious. How could he be abandoned? With whom rested the fault?

A daughter holds fault as a house holds a family. What a simple answer, and what a silly joke.

Now, the House arches tall in its creaking beams, watching once more. Seeking a flash of color beneath the branches, the shock of sunlight on metal, the car that did not approach the house. The traveler who understands the danger. The last Daughter's lover. Nothing came for the first Daughter, but times can change. Will change.

There. At the meadow's edge, just in the shadows. Her black curls, unwashed in her haste, waving over her round shoulders. Her plump face, crease worn deep between her brows, upturned to the attic windows. The House freezes. Dust motes halt in the air for a bare instant. The House must remind itself that it is not seen. The House has work to do.

The dogs patrol the field, the woods, the road. They are the earliest practice patterns of the Father's craft, rotting hovels driven by unloved doll-spirits. A newfound shame for the House. They skulk below the maples and prick their ears under the porch.

Why did the Father create them? To prove he could. Why does he keep them alive? Because they may yet be useful, as they were when the last Daughter attempted her escape. As they could be now, lifting their noses to the wind, peering through the bracken at the parked car that smells faintly of the last Daughter.

Crack. The House snaps off a piece of the front porch like teeth snapping through an elegant fingernail. Chunks of delicately carved railing tumble into the moss. Awareness of the break vibrates through the House, and in the basement, the Father raises his head.

"Beloved," he says to the cool air. "Is it rodents?"

The House taps inside the wall once. Yes. With a curled lip, the Father summons the dogs back to the House, disregarding the guests who cry out and dodge away from the sprinting creatures. The creatures—no longer quite dogs—sniff and sniff and sniff around the porch as the sun falls from the sky and the Daughter's lover settles into her car. The House drops curtains over windows that look out towards the woods. The House locks certain doors. And the Family notices nothing.

This is what the House can do. It folds the rest into the girls' hands. Into their palms, it delivers Fate like a baby bird fallen from its nest.

————

Lila, we'll be so infinitely lucky if all this works.

It's three minutes before the dolls are coming to collect me, and my knee is going like a piston under this ridiculous ruffly white dress. The long skirt looks innocent, and it covers up the knives I have taped to my thighs. Last night, I practiced ripping them free until my skin was tender and rashy. Then I dozed off for a few minutes and dreamed my fingers were clumsy lumps, fumbling to shreds against the blades. I woke up. I kept practicing.

I've told you the plan. The burner phone's battery icon is flashing, but I keep scrolling back through our texts, because—to be honest—it feels like they're the last communiques before a goddamn disaster.

You said: *5 p.m. Got it. I'll be outside the porch. Indecisive/lost tourist act.*

I said: *DO NOT go inside.*

You said: *I won't, as long as you come out.*

I couldn't type fast enough, cycling through the letters on each number pad, cursing if I overshot. *DONT. PROMISE ME. CALL COPS 4 BOMB SCARE.*

We can do this. I love you.

i love u 2.

One minute until the dolls come to collect me. The back of my skull pulses along the line of my missing scar. I flip the phone shut, shove it down my lace-trimmed sock until it's inside the patent leather shoe. It's uncomfortable, but that means it's fashion, right?

That would make you laugh. A hysterical, oh-God-oh-fuck laugh, but that counts.

I stand and smooth my silhouette in front of the mirror to make sure the contraband isn't too obvious. With my shadowed eyes and abysmal posture, I look like a haunted doll played by Boris Karloff.

You'd probably laugh at that one too. You've always been generous like that.

Bang! The closet door swings open and bounces off the dresser. I jump, hand flinching towards my thigh. Two dolls stand in the doorway. Mouse Father—his soft plush tense and twitchy—and the one I've seen the least, the Paper Father. His watercolor mouth arcs down, morose, and his eyes are a light, faded blue. His cardstock suit has aged edges, brown and brittle. My bedroom smells like a used bookstore as he shuffles forward.

"Best get a move on," he says, sweeping his arm in an after-you-please gesture. "Clock's ticking, dear."

I step past him, following Mouse Father into the elevator. This close, I can hear the wheezing squeaks he lets out with each breath. As the brass cage rises, we all scrunch together, shoulder to shoulder, although the Paper Father bends himself against the bars to take up less space. His sad eyes never leave me.

"We all want what's best for you," he says.

The knife's blade presses into my leg in a warm, sharp line. "That's why you're doing this?"

He nods once, crinkling.

The elevator jerks to a stop, but no one moves. Can Mouse Father feel the hard handle against his velvety side? My breathing tightens. Finally, Paper Father nods, and Mouse Father fumbles with a little gold key, opening the door to the blinding light of the skull.

Plastic Father raises his stiff arms in greeting. Through the eye windows, my own father looms above him like a bad moon, his gray eyes bright and bloodshot behind his glasses. I am brought to the control panel. Plastic Father adjusts a microphone on the console. No warmth or cold comes off his skin. I keep my gaze forward.

They have my dollhouse body sitting down, its wrists resting on a table cluttered with half-painted people and other deconstructions of life. My father stares at me with his jaw set in a *fuck-you* frown, his eyes not meeting mine—just the body's. Behind him, my mother remains perfectly motionless, blinking and smiling only when he glances at her.

Well? His voice rumbles through the skull, into my queasy belly. *Let's hear it.*

Lila, at this point, an apology to my parents is so far from the truth that it doesn't even feel like lying.

"I'm sorry." The body's voice repeats my words in a more cheerful tone, which is fucked-up. "I'm really sorry for what I did."

My dad leans back, crossing his thin arms. The father dolls shift around me, mimicking him as best they can with their half-jointed limbs, their crumpling paper elbows, their furred and stubby legs. Then, he reaches over. I tense.

But he just folds a daughter doll into the body's limp hands. Plastic Father and Mouse Father dance a complex choreography over the control panel—adjusting the fingers to cradle it, tilting the neck a few degrees for a better view—and I look through my old eyes at the unliving figure in my palm. She's around the size that I am now. If she was flesh and blood instead of carved wood, she'd be so easy to crush. Did my father hold me like this before he put me in the dollhouse? Is it easier to love something when you know you can destroy it? Does that count as love?

Lila, I think he's really trying to tell me something. I think he even means it. We sit side by side for a moment, me staring at the doll, thinking about all the times I came down here to wait with him while he worked. How I practiced laying my cheek on his arm as lightly as possible. How I practiced stillness, and he practiced—I don't know. I study the doll's sculpted curls and frilly skirt and dead blue eyes. Once, I heard my dad whisper, "I love you," to a doll he'd just finished painting, and I replayed those words in my tiny kindergarten brain until all I remembered was the remembering.

Dad takes back the doll with the tenderness of someone handling a newborn. *Okay.* He clears his throat. *You can put her away now.*

He lowers his jeweler's loupe, not looking at me. Behind him, my mom gives me a thumbs-up. My breathing shudders. Things happen between my quickening heartbeats.

Plastic Father gripping my arm too hard and hoisting me upright.

Mouse Father's curled paw at his waistcoat, pulling out the shiny gold key.

Paper Father starting to guide me, crinkling, to where the elevator cage waits to drop into darkness.

The three of us, leaving Plastic Father behind at the controls. Mouse Father lurching towards the elevator, panting.

And me, stepping. Pretending to lose my balance, falling forward. Crumpling, my fingertips already on the knife. Knowing the weight of the handle in my palm, knowing my practice, knowing that I'll never want to tell you this. Knowing that I can and I will.

Paper Father, laying one hand light as a paperback page on my back.

Me, thinking, *Go.*

I explode up, the tape tearing free from my skin, everything slow and shimmering at the edges. Paper Father's face folds and fragments between my clawing, clenching fingers, and the knife glints when it catches in his neck, just next to the painted line of his Adam's apple.

Paper rips. A timeworn eye fixes on me. He doesn't even look upset as his body collapses to the floor. When I release his head, it floats down like an autumn leaf, staring up sightlessly.

Mouse Father screams, a long, panicked, animal shriek. Plastic Father is yelling too, a string of curses crackling from his throat, and—and my own father's voice booms out. *Get her back upstairs.*

For a second, I freeze, but I make myself remember: *he can't see me.* I lunge, seizing Mouse Father's tail and dragging him back, wrapping my arm under his velvety chin and holding the bloodless knife to his throat. He goes motionless. His breath comes in hot little squeaks between his yellow teeth.

The plan is working. I'm not dead yet. Plastic Father, standing stoic beside the control panel with his hands raised, watches us.

"I won't hurt him if I don't have to," I say. Mouse Father struggles, but he's weak, full of rice and cotton. My heartbeat thumps through my sweaty palm into the knife's grip. My voice trembles. "You're going to walk upstairs, and you're going to take this body outside. Got it?"

Plastic Father leans back against the control panel, lets his arms dangle loose. One articulated finger taps against the metal. Even under the high dome of the skull, he's too large. "You're making a terrible mistake, little missy."

I stick the point of the knife into a seam until the old stitches start to give. Mouse Father squirms and whimpers.

A staticky sigh from Plastic Father, but his permanent smile doesn't shift. "You should have picked Mr. Paper." He straightens up. "We had better conversations."

He slams a lever forward, and we all rocket off our feet. In my hand, the blade tears stupid and aimless through Mouse Father's throat, spraying rice grains. The view of the basement through the body's eyes whirls, growing larger, and I slam into the glass, fist-sized rice pelting me like rocks. Next to me, Mouse Father rasps, his paws scratching feebly at the floor, button eyes still bright but emptying. I groan, crouch—where's the knife—and a grip like God's wraps around my neck.

My fingers scrabble at the huge rubbery hand as it lifts me. I gurgle, air fleeing, vision fuzzing, feet kicking at empty air. Plastic Father folds me in to face him, to study me with his dead eyes. There are pink circles painted on his cheeks, and even those are fading as thumb and forefinger crush me.

Lila, I'm sorry. I'm so sorry. I've loved you so much.

I hear you call my name, and I'm glad my brain gives me this.

But then, in my blackened vision, Plastic Father's smile widens, and oh God—

You've come into the house.

The House remembers love. Fathers and Mothers in their warm beds, laughing. Holding the fussing Baby at mealtimes, passing him back and forth so they can both eat while the food is hot. Checking that none of the candles are close to the curtains. Kissing red-faced children on their foreheads. Watching the same children make their first attempts at courtship out on the wide porch. Giggling together as though young again. Children, grown, guiding the Mother with cataracts around the icy walk, laying flowers on the Father's grave so he can rest easy. The lives repeating through treasured summers and drowsy winters, up to the newest Mother kissing her baby Daughter's tiny fists as the child bawled.

The House remembers love even in the early days, when the Mother grew thin and the Father draped his coat over her and the Son and the Daughter. When the Son lay fever-sick and death-shaking in the loft, and the Mother laid snow-soaked cloths on his insensible skin, and the Father asked the Daughter to look upon him, and he didn't even have to speak for her to understand. The bones forcing the edges of the Son's skin were enough.

And the Father sharpened the knife with love. And the Daughter followed him, a loyal firstborn lamb, into the cellar with love. Her hands on his trembling hands. Her mouth on God's words. And God didn't speak to save her.

And the knife came down with love.

In the guilty, turned-away eyes, love shone. In the Mother's red hand and the Son's stinging cheek, love burned. In the throat that swallowed tears, love did not drown. Love was patient; it waited for happier lives as the high-collared Daughter waited amongst the dollhouses her Father built for her. Love was kind; it forgave to be forgiven. The Son became the Father standing at his own Father's grave, wondering if he'd stayed away too long. The Mother soothed the crying Daughter, hoping the Daughter would one day comfort her in turn.

Was it love, then? The last Father planning, laboring, building as all his forefathers had? Loving in their name, in their House? The last Mother believing that love lay in the sameness of each day, in the waiting for wildflowers, in the settling of the House into her own grave? The last

Daughter returning, clear-eyed and immediately blinded, as her Father had once returned?

Yes. Yes, it was love.

Love like a hand around the throat. Love like a meal-time of air. Love like the empty space on a tombstone, the marble promise of a coming death.

But then, the Daughter's lover: seeing the front door crash open into the darkness of the House's screaming and empty throat, rushing forward regardless of known dangers, burying herself in the once-arms of the Daughter? Is that love?

Of an unknown kind, perhaps. Yes.

The House remembers love. And I recognize it now.

––––––––

Your scream: *Birdie!*

Plastic Father drops me, and I crumple. Limbs aren't listening. Fingers fumble across polished bone. Eyes blurred, throat burned—I think I'm dead for a second, but being dead can't hurt this much, and if I'm dead, then I can't help you, so I can't be dead, Lila. I can't.

I haul myself onto my elbows, breath whistling through my strangled throat. Something whooshes, and a foot buries in my belly. I collapse. On my side, I heave coffee and stomach acid across Plastic Father's shoe. He stares at me, his hatted head shadowed against the wide eyes behind him, where—*Lila.*

You're facing away, the many houses of the basement towering over you. You raise a bat over your shoulder. The one from your *A League of Their Own* Halloween costume. Our first date. Your hair is tied back, and all your sun-freckles are standing out. You need to wear sunscreen. I love you so much. My parents stand apart from you, at the other end of the room, cowering like two normal, frail people. You don't give them shit. *Stay back! Don't come near us! We're leaving!*

In the skull, I claw my way forward, and Plastic Father kicks me again, a lazy, glancing strike across the temple that sends me down a third time. My vision pops and sparkles.

"You've done this to yourself," he says.

His stride *thunk*-drags-*thunk*-drags across the floor towards the console. Furniture screeches over the floor as he shoves it out of his path. I breathe in through my nose, out through my mouth. Focus. He's limping. One of his thighs is disjointed. He hurt himself in the fall. I raise my head, unsteady, searching. The knife glints a few feet away, caught beneath one of the desks. I wriggle forward, trying to get my legs under me, still too dizzy to go as fast I need to.

Birdie, you say, and I stagger forward, faster. *Birdie, are you in there? It's time to go!*

"Yes," Plastic Father says, and my own voice echoes him, chiming through the basement air. I stare, one hand halfway to the knife. Plastic Father's hands tap a series of buttons, close on levers. "Yes, sweetheart, I'm here."

Your smile. Your relief, your crooked front tooth, your shining eyes. You reach to embrace me. I reach for the knife. Plastic Father pushes the levers forward, and hands that aren't mine catch you by the throat.

I want to say that I cross the room without realizing it. That when we're old and gray and talking about this late at night, I'll tell you that I still don't remember moving. That I grew wings to fly to you. But I don't.

Lila, my legs are slow underneath me. The knife is slick in my sweaty hand. My shaky steps unbalance me, whirl the room into a carousel, and your terrorized face is the only thing I see, filling the body's gaze and mine with your wide eyes and gasping mouth and the realization that hits far too late, and I stumble, and I rise, and I run towards Plastic Father. And my thumbs are digging into your neck, and your fingers are clawing pink lines into my hands, and I scream like you're trying to scream when your brown eyes drift towards your forehead and Plastic Father leans into the controls, and I jump onto his wide shoulders, and I bring the knife down and it hardly scores his plastic suit, and his hand sinks into my bicep, and I'm spinning through the air for a moment, but if he's killing me it means that he's not killing you, and that's enough for me, Li.

He has me around the neck again. I'm kicking. I think I'm even smiling, wheezing out: "So, this is like your thing, huh?"

It gets to him, Lila. He drags me in close even though he could just snap me in half and be done with it. In the background, you're free—coughing, wheezing, shrieking at my parents, *Get away! Don't fucking touch her!* Plastic Father's face shines oddly, flickering. Something's wrong with the lights outside. Distant doors slam and slam and slam. My fingertips are going numb. In my fading vision, Plastic Father's grin warps into a snarl.

I stab him in the eye.

Swinging gleam of the knife up. Slashing glitter of the knife down. Crunch. *Squish.*

He's not supposed to go squish. He trips backwards, his dislocated leg wobbling, and he has to catch himself. His grip loosens for a second, and he stares up at me, blue iris severed around the blade. A trickle of something pink pools there, falls like tears. I dangle in his hand, gasping, my fist still clenched around the knife.

His smile is as wide as ever, as if the snarl had never happened. "You'll have to do better than that, sport."

"Yeah," I agree, choking, and slam my shiny leather shoe into his wounded hip.

Plastic Father buckles, twisting into the fall, and I move with him, both hands on the knife now, my eyes on his, the control panel rushing up behind him. Blue-white sparks shower from the thin metal as the controls sheer and splinter beneath him, arcing hot around his face, his mouth splitting, melting, finally opening in an agonized howl. Lila—I watch him die.

The lights burn out on the control panel. The machines whine to a stop. Flashing basement lights filter in through the body's half-lidded windows. From the broken levers, a few sparks pop, eye-scarringly bright in the gloom. I slide the knife free of Plastic Father. The blade drips with rosy goop. My exhausted breathing is loud, but your voice outside is louder. *Birdie, answer me! Birdie!*

I approach the microphone on the control panel. It's smoking. Of course it's smoking. I lean over to dig my phone out of my Mary Janes and nearly fall as the whole room spins again. I manage to call you without passing out.

I drag myself along the wall to the barely open eye window, nudging past Mouse Father's emptied bag of a body. You're brandishing the bat one-handed now. My parents creep forward, caught in strobing flashes. Alongside the slamming doors and your ringing cell phone, I hear the dogs howl. Shit.

Your panicked voice crackles in my ear. "Birdie?"

"I'm alive." I can barely push words out of my ragged throat. "Can't move the body. Controls—" I stare at the inert mound of Plastic Father's corpse. "Controls broke."

"Birdie—" my mother calls, her voice weak. "Sweetie, please—"

"Don't talk to her!" You swing the bat in a wide arc, and my mom's feet shuffle a couple steps back. My dad stands motionless in his house slippers. After a childhood spent listening for him, I catch him murmuring among the terrible noise of the house. But he's not talking to me.

Do this for me. Please, just this last thing. Please, protect us.

You don't hear it. When you next speak, your voice is low, gentle. "I'm going to get you to the car."

"The dogs—"

"I know. We'll figure it out." The body heaves, and I clutch the wall. You're pulling me up the stairs. Christ, you're strong.

The dogs are getting louder. Wood crunches and splinters. You say, "I love you, Bird."

My eyes sting. "I love you too."

"*Fine,*" Dad bellows, his voice ringing from the walls, and maybe I should have told you about the muttering after all. "I'll do it myself."

He crumples. His skull cracks against the stones. Mom screams. You swear, your voice doubling through the phone, *What the fuck?* I press my face against the window. I can't breathe. His blood shines. It spreads in a glimmering spiderweb across the mortar.

Something reflects in the eye's lens, shifting behind me.

At the console, Plastic Father sits up.

———

I wake into myself and watch the last Son's soul spring golden from his body. I wake into myself, and the last Son spills onto the floor, bones age-rotten, brain burning down with blood, an attic aflame. I wake into myself as I have not done in centuries, eyes rolling sightless in their multitudes, mouths crushed jagged in their toothy abundance, hands twist-knuckling a boneyard into being. I am house, body, soul. A creature of corners, a beast embedded in intricate locks, a million throats roaring tongueless hymns—an awful, beautiful daughter.

When my father killed me, and I failed to die, I thought it would be enough if I were both barren and fruitful. Aren't all angels impossible beings? If I helped my family build and build and build, I thought it would be enough. Lord, I believed that I had made a city on a hill with a million loving, painted eyes, but it was only ever empty dwellings within empty dwellings, and I was only ever the sacrificial blood consecrating a curse. I was never meant for a blessing. Alive, I was only an inconvenient mouth. Dead, I was even less.

What have I done?

I was not a comfort for the lonely woman now wailing over her husband, nor for the shattered man rising in his daughter's skull, nor for the terrified girl glancing between her lover and the father she never understood.

What have I done.

No. What can I do.

It can't be nothing.

———

Plastic Father drags himself up from the console, long strings of melted plastic stretching from his ruined head to the sparking metal. He touches the back of his skull, fingertips feeling out the architecture of disaster.

I curl against a desk. Plastic Father's uneven footfalls cross the room, and I peek over the furniture. Past toppled desks and disorderly chairs, the doll towers beside the narrow elevator door. He examines the interior, then straightens, surveying the skull. I duck.

"Bridget," Plastic Father says, and I press my hands to my mouth, swallow my whimpers. His voice is resonant, hoarse, and completely empty of static. My father's voice. "Bridget, you're still here, aren't you?"

I'm still here. And so is Dad.

His steps drag over the floor, faint but growing louder. My whole body trembles. My eyes dart to Mouse Father across the room. His paws curl, rigid, over his collapsed waistcoat. He had the key to the elevator. He still has it—he better still have it—but he's out in the open, way too visible.

Dad grunts, and metal crashes, high and screeching and shattering against the floor. I flinch. Bits of the delicate machinery that monitored my dollhouse body roll under the desk, past my shiny black shoes.

He hasn't seen me, because he's not lunging for me. He just wants me to think that he's seen me. He doesn't even really know if I'm here—he just has faith that he can scare me shitless. He wants me to run. I keep my streaming eyes wide, force my hands into stillness around the knife and the cell phone. I synchronize my breaths with yours, Lila. You haven't hung up, and your breathing is loud through the phone and my once-body's ears as you haul it up the stairs, louder even than the scratching, snarling dogs and the incomprehensible racket of the house.

I have to get the key from Mouse Father, and I have to do it without being seen.

If my dad thinks he knows where I am, then he won't look to see where I'm not.

I whisper into the phone, praying you have it close to your ear. "Lila. Don't say anything."

Your breath hitches, and outside the eye window, your arm tightens around my chest. You've heard me. The body's head lolls, and everything in the skull screeches a few inches to the right. I brace myself against the desk to keep from sliding over the tilting floor.

"I'm in trouble," I say. Somewhere behind me, Dad topples the shelf of computers. Plastic crunches, glass explodes in glittering music, and I draw my knees up to my chin. "I need you to call this phone in one minute. Say 'okay' if you got it."

"Okay," you murmur, and your face must be right next to my ear, because that word reverberates through the floor and up into my chest. I press my cheek into the phone, then close it. *One. Two. Three.* I gather myself, one foot set like a sprinter at the starting line, ready to go.

Dad flings an office chair across the room, and the desk—my hiding place—cracks with a sound like splitting firewood. I cringe into the ivory floor. I can't move. Dad's footsteps thump louder still, confused into the noise of my heartbeat and the slamming doors.

"Stop being a child and *come out.*" His voice seems to hiss just behind my ear. I shudder, squeeze my eyes shut, but no one grabs me, and his next words are more distant. "Come out and fix this."

Outside, Mom sobs. I've lost count of how much time has passed. Twenty seconds? Thirty? I move—finally—like a bad dream, endlessly crawling forward, my attention gathered between my shoulder blades. I'm a spider waiting for a hand to smash it. You heave me upwards, and the floor pitches again. I slip over smooth bone, clutch heavy furniture legs to remain stable.

I wriggle under a desk past giant rice grains, my breath heavy, my head still twinging each time I lower it. When an overturned table shifts and groans with another sudden angling of my skull, I brace myself against its legs. I curl as small as possible beside the filing cabinets as Dad passes too close.

What will he do if he catches me?

No time to think about it. I slide the phone across the gleaming floor to a hidden spot deep beneath a desk. Dad is next to the elevator again, puppy-guarding. His hat shadows his face, but he can't see me skulking and shaking in the warren of tables and cabinets. I once thought he could always see me, but that was before I started crawling out of windows to kiss girls. Before I kept secret phones. Before I ran away, and got away, and stayed away for so long. I can do it again. I am strong enough and smart enough to do it again, and you're here with me this time—so it'll be easy, right?

Mouse Father is just ahead of me now, pale polyfill stuffing caught in wisps on his long yellow teeth. A loop of silk ribbon emerges from his waistcoat, and a tiny bit of brass winks in the light—the key. I switch the knife to my left hand. Flex my fingers.

Through the crowded noise of doors and dogs, of my mom's sobs and your steady breaths, the cell phone's ringing cuts like a baby's scream. Dad's head whips towards the shrill techno burble. He strides towards it, climbing over desks, shoving aside filing cabinets that shriek as their bolts rip from the bone. I creep to Mouse

Father's corpse, my head spinning from the momentum—Christ, Lila, I'm fucked-up—and I slip my wrist through the ribbon on the second try, and I wobble towards the elevator, so close, so close.

And the phone goes silent.

I freeze. Dad can't have found it already. He can't have answered it. And he hasn't. A desk crashes over, a static-filled voice roars, *"Bridget!"*

But Lila, you say, "Shit," and you say, "Birdie, the phone—"

I understand. The call dropped. The phone's finally dead. I understand, and my father understands it, too, the distraction of it all, and across the skull, he stretches to his full height. He turns in a slow swivel, and his gaze catches me halfway to the elevator. The windows throw pulsing light over his face. One of his painted eyes is just gone, melted into twisted plastic that drags his smile into a dripping grimace.

I dive for the door, finding the lock as my eyesight kaleidoscopes into blurs and sparkles. I jam the key home as my father screams for me. Fling open the door. Furniture splinters somewhere behind me. White-knuckle the doorframe when the room shifts again, the body's head falling onto your shoulder, buying me time. I tumble inside with the floor shaking, swear I feel fingers brush my wrist as I slam the barrier shut between him and me, and definitely feel the impact as he smashes into the wall once—twice—again and again. It must be wood over shaped bone, because otherwise he'd already be through. I slump against the warm bars of the descending elevator and close my eyes.

Of course, I hadn't really felt his hand on my wrist, Lila. It was just a remnant of that last night in the basement, a decade gone. The chain clinks as Dad continues to batter down my skull.

————

Except for me, the children aren't dead yet. Good.

I pull myself away from high windows watching the sunset, through dog-bashed doors, through creaking hardwood. Down into the basement. But I do not bring myself to where I knelt that last day, braiding my hair and waiting for the knife.

I bring myself to the corner where I undid my bandages and studied the toothmarks of the dog, the one I freed from the trap. By candlelight, I marveled at the punctures, the worried, reddened flesh. A weak and wounded creature had made me bleed, had fled stumbling into the wilderness. My brother found me there, asked me, You regret it, don't you? with his wide eyes shining in the single flame. I only stared at the bloody marks, as though a witch's child had suckled at my palm. I only regretted not following the dog deeper into the forest.

I was never meant to be a house. I was meant to be wind through grass, light through smoke. The brief heat of a kiss.

Now, I lay my lips against my hand. In the corner of the basement, an unheard breath, an unseen spark. Among the forgotten dollhouses, no larger than a candle, a fire burns.

————

Somewhere outside, the body rumbles and shifts, and the reverberations shudder through the dollhouse. The elevator scrapes the side of the throat, rolls over an invisible edge, and falls. I curl up—*Lila Lila Lila*—and hold on. The landing bounces me into the air. I cling to the bottom of the elevator, groaning as the cage settles at the bottom of my dark throat. The chain pools musically atop the bars.

I hope you're almost out. I hope you've somehow befriended those dogs, because I want one of us to be doing okay, and I am really not doing okay.

I paw at the brass bars. Aside from my raggedy, whimpery breathing and the slow drag of blood through my big body's veins, it's quiet. All the noise that let me know that you were near—that the house is freaking out—is gone. Dad crashes, muffled, into the wall upstairs.

The dollhouse trembles again, and I catch myself as I slip. Christ, Lila—please be okay. I shoulder the battered gate open, fumble with the door key in the dark.

I have no idea how I'm going to get to you. If the hostage situation had gone as planned—and how the hell did I ever think that was going to work—I would have booted the other fathers out of the skull and worked from there. Popped out an eyeball or busted open the nasal cavity or, per your preference, just lockpicked my forehead. You, me, and one of your infinite bobby pins. But I can't go back in the skull now, and I can't afford to hide.

The key clunks into the lock as another impact from Dad rumbles down the elevator shaft. Where could I hide, anyway? I push the door open, hesitating at the threshold and blinking in the closet's artificial light. He built this place.

New sound. *Crunch.* A cluster of somethings clatters down my throat, clangs off the elevator bars as I shield my head. A bloody shingle-sized chunk bounces off the floor. Splintered bone gleams, and my eyes widen. Fuck—

Dad slams into the elevator. Fragile brass shrieks under his plastic bulk, his kicking feet and scrabbling hands. His overly jointed fingers grab and grab and grab at my hair through the bars, but I've already dropped to the floor, already crawled onto the closet's carpet and collapsed, my head pounding.

At the top of the door, his pale fingers emerge from the darkness to rip at the doorframe's pristine molding. From the jagged cavity in the rose-patterned wallpaper, his new face looms, a crescent of oozing cheekbone and eye. He's too large for the gap, too large for the house. His eye swivels. Shining, searching. I scramble farther away, seize the bottoms of the doll dresses, accidentally shred a couple with the knife I won't let go of, and use them to haul myself upright. Mom's perfume wafts from them.

"Bridget," Dad says.

I stop. Lila, it's his voice for dolls. Soft and sorry as rain. The one he only uses when nobody alive—nobody who can hurt him—is listening. The one I followed him around the house to hear.

"You've never understood." His luminous gray eye twitches in its socket, finds my face. It glimmers, blood-shot and wet and *alive* in a way that the Plastic Father's never was, and I'm paralyzed watching it. I want to be small like the dolls are small, small in a way that's safe. His melted smile unfastens. His words rasp through a fleshy web. "Bridget. I know I didn't come upstairs, but you didn't come down. Please."

Dad strains forward, softened plastic pulling back from new white teeth, fresh and bloodied ivory sprouting from rubbery gums. He reaches out again, but not to snatch at me. No. He offers me his hand. Plastic palm up, articulated fingers twitching. The last time I saw him do this, I was halfway to busting my head open.

"You can still understand," he breathes.

"Absolutely fucking not," I say, and flee from my childhood bedroom with my father roaring behind me.

———

The fire eats, crackling through the dollhouse living room, consuming the kitchen, leaping from balsa-wood windows to the house next door. Bright flames lash sparks against blackening dormers and incinerate curlicued trim into spiraling red embers. All that paper. Cardboard. Old, dry wood. Already, the ceiling shimmers with heat.

Elsewhere, I hold fast against the no-longer-dogs howling on the porch. I turn locks. I lift windows and let in the wind. I rattle pipes and burst lights and slam doors of all sizes in the houses. In the meadow, grass grows overlong on the family graves. The clouds trace their slow voyage across the sky.

And I am burning down.

The newcomer—the friend—the lover—no, her name is Lila—has the doll-stiff Daughter halfway up the stairs and doesn't yet see the fire. Her eyes are too intent on the Daughter's empty face. The Mother—Connie—notices it first, turning from her husband. Her hands tighten on his cooling shoulders. Her tear-stained cheeks gleam orange.

I topple a shelf, and forgotten dolls burst from archival boxes. They pour over the stones, fleeing in their own ways. I swing the basement door open. In the porch's late sunlight, a not-collie shreds its unliving mouth as it gnaws the doorframe. At the sight of flames leaping from shelf to shelf, Lila falls back, groaning with effort, dragging the Daughter upwards.

Connie holds the Father close to her bloodied breast, stares up at Lila with a desperate expression. "Help me," she says. "Please, help me."

A few dark curls stick to Lila's forehead, joined by early ash. She grits her teeth.

In the attic, the Barbies skip out of their Dreamhouses. Pewter and paper dolls fall and float from the Victorians. Suburban families snap free from old glue and dash past their white picket fences. I hold the windows wide, making the glass my palms and fingertips.

Lila knows she's going to help. She props the Daughter's body at the top of the stairs. Best not to jostle the Daughter inside. She crosses to Connie, takes hold of the Father's skinny, socked ankles, and by accident burns the image of his head wound into her memory. Blood the color of late summer plums. Flames ring the two women, light their faces with shadowed gold. A magnification of the candles my brother once carried into the sunless cellar.

"Thank you," Connie says. Her lips form the words in a perfect feat of levers and buttons.

"Don't talk to me," Lila answers.

At the attic window, the first dolls soar into the sky.

———

I limp through the halls at top speed, which is—guess what—way too slow.

Dad busted through my cranium, so there's no way a wispy little elevator will hold him for that long. I've got nowhere to go: none of the doors in the house are doors, none of the windows in the house are windows. The only exit wound I've managed to make is the size of my fist and snarled behind gunky plaster and rotten wood and scabbed-up blood. I didn't even break my skin, didn't see daylight. I lean against the tilted walls and let gravity drag me forward in a lurching jog.

Maybe it would have been smarter to take his hand. Let him be the father he thinks he is. But I know where that leads. Down the basement stairs, *crack*, onto the basement floor. At least there'd be no stones for me to land on this time.

And, oh my God, Lila—I'm an idiot.

They keep telling me to stay out of the basement.

Rending metal shrieks down the hallway, and I pump my stumbling legs faster. Elevator's gone. A wretched crunching—drywall, crumbling like mummified remains—follows. I swing myself around the banister at the top of the stairs, aim for a leap onto the landing, settle for flailing and an aching wrist when I hit the hardwood.

I have to get to the basement, Lila, because if the basement doesn't have a floor, if the basement doesn't have walls, if the basement isn't *actually* part of the dollhouse, then, well—then it's just meat.

The knife in my hand flashes silver as I push myself upright again, trembling. I slouch down the next set of stairs, counting the familiar planks as I go. Nearly there. Nearly. The floors shake. I hope it's you, dragging me along, quaking through bones and muscle and hardwood damp with blood.

Wrong. It's Dad. "Bridget!"

I look, and he's there. Looming at the top of the stairs, but crashing downwards, shoulders scraping the ceiling, hands clawing forward. Ripping through wallpaper, gouging out plaster until his jointed fingertips snap backwards, until they twist at the knuckles, until his thumbs shear past the screws and dangle, useless. I half-dash, half-dive away from him. A huge hand, wire armatures sprouting from degloved rubber flesh, swipes through empty air. Scraps of dangling plastic brush my bruised cheek. I can't breathe.

I lunge sideways, too fast, vertigo spinning the walls into floral nonsense, and end up in the parlor. Puffs of blood stench erupt as I crush the scabbed carpet below my hands and knees and scramble to my feet. I glance back, because I have to, because I've spent my whole life watching out for this man. He's pulling himself through the door, through the wall, his shoulders crushed out of their joints as the doorframe bulges around them, his wounded leg dragging at a senseless angle. Too huge for the house he's made.

But then he looks at me, and he *hates* me, Lila. His face a death mask twisted rigid with rage, his toothed mouth open and howling around a flesh-bubbling, half-formed tongue. His eye a single silver fire.

I don't look back again, not when the wood groans and shatters, not when footsteps shake the floor and the smell of gore intensifies, not when Dad snarls at me to be anything other than a disappointment, to make this right, to stop killing the house, killing my mother, killing him. I duck past the bloodstained couch where I sat to watch the wall-wound bleed.

I make it to the kitchen. The broken window's image shivers between its cracks, trying to remake itself. Globs of blackened oatmeal splatter the counter and walls beside the emptied pot. Plates have tumbled out of their cabinets and shattered on the scab floor. Fresh blood seeps around the shards.

"*Bridget.*" My father's voice is higher now, pained.

I still don't look back. I keep my eyes on the basement door, its faint ring of pulsing light. I seize the doorknob.

————

I expect it to hurt. Is that not the curse of the body, a lifetime of suffering in exchange for relief? But yet again, I am wrong. Pain and Joy answer the same door for living souls, but my ghostly self no longer knocks. I was not wounded when the Victorian Daughter—when Emily tried to join me behind the walls. And I am not injured now.

The basement towers with fire, and I grow lighter. I pull myself down to the dolls surging over the tiles, taking flight up the banisters. I drift beside Lila as she hurries away from the flames, one of the Father's legs in each hand, and beside Connie as she cradles her husband's head and shoulders against her chest. Strands of silver hair fall from her bun and brush his lined, blood-smeared forehead.

Lila hefts the Father's feet higher and backs up the narrow steps. Dolls glide on warm thermals past her cheeks, their arms spread wide, coattails and dresses trembling like banners. Her brown eyes flick to them for an instant and then turn again to Connie, whose arms do not shake, whose eyes are unblinking in the smoke.

They pass the last Daughter's body where she waits like a corpse on display. Two blue crescent moons stare sightless through her translucent eyelashes, and Lila swallows.

"Oh." Connie pauses, looking at her daughter. "Oh, my baby."

Sparks leap to the dry wood of the staircase. Lila tugs on the Father's ankles, guiding the parents forward, glaring at them both. "She's like this because of you. She's hurt because of you."

The Father's cracked head rolls across his wife's apron and leaves a bloody trail as Connie stumbles after Lila. Connie's soft, wrinkled hands seem to be wearing crimson gloves.

"You don't understand," Connie says.

Lila bites her tongue, concentrates on passing through the door without catching on the Daughter's claw-tensed fingers. I know she wants to say that she doesn't want to get it, that she hopes she never gets it. I hope so too—I pray she never understands as I have understood. I've made certain that my windows close tight against cold drafts, and I've hovered over every familial dispute with the dead certainty of total understanding. I was an angel praising cold glory, inconsolable abandonment, and I was wrong. I wonder if God also fails to comprehend His children's minds. I hope so. I hope that we are still capable of surprising God.

Dad calls to me, and I wonder if he knows what I'm doing.

I open the basement door.

The smell of my flesh rolls over me, wounded salt. Old wooden steps, glittering wet, point down to the light and the literal pit in my gut. That single lightbulb flares bright around the scarlet blood spatters. It swings, casting wild shadows over the viscera-dripping staircase that hangs alone over the black abyss.

And, at the very edge of its glow: a rosy shiver. A red pulse.

I sprint down, staying upright, splashing through accumulated gore that sprays off the narrow sides. I fling myself forwards from the sticky, splintery handrail. Swallowing myself. Nine steps. Six steps. Three steps.

Footfalls—heartbeats—breaths. Heavy like I can never run fast enough, like my dreams of the house closing around me. Lungs burning, misted with my own blood. Eyes fixing ahead. Knife flashing. Dad's broken fingers scrape and slide over my shoulder. He can't hold me. He cries out for me to wait, and he means it.

Red rain jellies from the ceiling, plummets into the shadows.

One step.

I love you, Lila.

I jump.

The dolls jump from every window, darkening the twilight sky like a flock of migrating birds. Outside, a golden not-dog looks up and snarls, the toy people inside its cramped skull screaming, "Traitors, traitors." Another of the not-dogs—the smallest—sprints for the forest. Two more bring it down, teeth vicious in tendoned legs, in glass eyes. I creak, split porch railings, burst windows in glittering showers over their heads. They do not listen to me.

Lila sets the Father's death-heavy legs down in the front hallway and fetches the Daughter from the nook at the top of the basement stairs, shivering as her fingers slip over the unyielding hinges embedded in her lover's ribs. The lowermost steps are fully ablaze now. Dollhouse roofs fall in gouts of tall fire. Flames pound like bright hands against the underside of the kitchen floor. Lila turns her face from the heat.

In the breakfast nook, dolls leave their meals to burn with relief. Paper dolls flutter and tumble in the smoke, colorful ephemera. In the small not-dog's skull and the Daughter's belly, dolls scream. Lila cannot hear them as she hauls her lover towards the front door. It trembles as a not-dog hurls itself into the wood, howling its fury.

Connie waits for a pulse in the Father's neck, kneeling on the coal-hot boards of the front hallway. Lila stumbles back towards her, sweaty, holding the Daughter like a shipwrecked sailor clutching a spar.

"How do we get past the dogs?" Lila asks. Connie smooths darkening blood from her husband's grizzled eyebrows.

The smallest not-dog, glass eyes weeping shards, slips free and stumbles again towards the woods. I slam shutters, break pipes, shatter each porch light—calling with my many mouths until the pursuers at last turn back to witness me.

"Hey!" Lila says. "How do we get out? Can't you call 911 or something?"

Connie, who knows she is the last Mother, looks up. Tears have left clean pink tracks through the soot on her face. I do not know if the Father gave her vessel the ability to cry, or if, by some magic of her own, she's refashioned this tiny part of herself. "I've wanted this place to burn down for years."

Her mouth doesn't move when she says it. Oh, my enemy. I'm sorry I've taken so long to realize the same.

The smallest not-dog bursts through the ferns and disappears into the land beyond.

Connie stands, her eyes—the Daughter's eyes, Lila realizes with a twisting stomach—now studying Lila for the first time, flicking up and down her body. Studying her curly hair that's come free from its tie, the tattoos spread over her skin, the circumference of her waist and upper arms. "You're the kind of girl my daughter likes?"

"I'm the girl your daughter loves," Lila snaps. She coughs out lungfuls of hot, bitter air. "Tell me how to get us out of here."

The dolls spiral above the house, riding the heat higher and higher. The not-dogs scratch at the porch as black smoke winds around their paws. They bite and claw at the door as the foundation relaxes into the flames.

Connie nods. "I'm sure you're very nice."

Connie walks to the front door and unlocks it as Lila screams for her to stop, as I shift myself from the not-dogs. Connie turns the doorknob, and I twist the deadbolt too late, and Lila, half-gasping and half-sobbing, pulls the Daughter away. Connie and I watch the not-dogs flood in as Lila's face turns to despair.

———

Lila. I'm seventeen years old, and I'm bleeding on the basement floor, staring up at my father. He's not looking at me.

A few minutes ago, I refused to go into the basement. Late summer. The crickets singing through the window, the fireflies winking and dancing all across the meadow. A girl—M.K. Taylor—waiting for me in the woods. School newly started up again, my backpack swung over one shoulder.

The lie about going out on the porch to do homework was sweet and easy. The kitchen smelled like basil from dinner, and I'd eaten a slice of angel food cake for dessert. Mom was putting the rest of it away with her back to me, and Dad had just told me to go down into the basement and finish the project he'd had me doing since May, dammit, and I'd said, "No."

"What do you mean, no?" He held the basement door open, his arm blocking me like a gate.

"I have homework." Anger snapped, firecrackers up my slouching spine. I straightened, glaring down at this bitter little man. Three summers I'd been in the basement for kissing a girl. He didn't even know what I'd managed to get up to since then. "Can't I do homework?"

Mom murmured, "She has homework."

"She needs to finish what she starts," Dad snarled.

Over his shoulder, I spotted the brief spark of headlights through the trees—oh, Christ, what if he saw them—and I said, "Fuck this," and I shoved between Dad and the door, and—

He pushed me. Hand high and hard against my sternum, sudden awareness of my ribs. Stumble back, one foot cascading heel, arch, toes down the basement stairs, the other slipping backwards over the first step. A gasping stomach-drop shift in gravity. My soul catching up with my body, my gaze finding the ceiling. I fell.

But not for very long. I jerked to a halt, my shoulder aching. My father's wiry hand clenched, bruising, around my wrist. I couldn't see Mom. My breathing was all gasps. Sick scared puppy breaths. Dad held me, barely balanced. His gray eyes, intense behind thumb-printed glasses, held me too.

"You reached for me," he said, unsurprised. His frown-lined mouth barely opened as he spoke. "Do you understand what that means?"

And then, Lila—then, he let go.

Connie opens the door, and Lila despairs, and the not-dogs surge. Fur and teeth, stitches and bad magic. My many hands in all of it. I slam open the coat closet door, collide with a limping not-dog and send it spinning backwards. Lila holds the Daughter close, gasping smoke as she tries to run. I flicker lights—here, this way, this way!—back through the hall, to the drawing room. I catch a not-dog with another door, trapping it inside a cleaning cupboard with old mops and scrubbing brushes. I blow out chandelier lights, and the not-dogs skid over glass. I buckle the floor into the burning basement. The not-dogs leap. One of them plummets. A plume of red sparks. Scent of burning fur and glue. The others do not look back. Air shines with ashen heat, but the lungs in my walls are summer-filled, sun-fueled.

Lila follows the blinking lights to the tower, panting, coughing. She crosses the threshold. The not-dogs snap at the Daughter's toes. I hold myself in the door, crashing closed just shy of the not-dogs' dry noses. In safety—what passes for safety in this house—Lila and the Daughter tumble to the floor. Wild-eyed, singe-palmed, Lila scans the room and finds no windows on the ground floor, no doors, only walls thick with odd dollhouses—a kettle, a typewriter, a doll's head, how familiar—and the spiral staircase at the center of the room. Dolls climb up the stairs like mice, crawl over the houses like bats, take flight from the narrow, faraway windows like angels.

The rug smolders. I am in the beams below, groaning and weakening. I am in the deadbolt of the door, shuddering with the impacts of the not-dogs. I am sparking the light fixtures that I cast into shards of glass days ago, calling without any voice. I am at the wall with Lila, struggling to hold Birdie upright as the heat rises and the room boils like a stew pot. I am slumping with Lila onto the hardwood, and I am leaping with the Daughter inside her stomach, and I am standing with the Father on the crumbling dollhouse stairs, and I am watching Connie watch me burn, her blue eyes all orange in reflected flames.

Connie is waiting for the not-dogs to finish their work. Waiting to run for the Daughter inside, if there's time. In her mind, there has to be time. But only two not-dogs scratch at the door, and the hardwood is succumbing to hellfire. As the flames embrace the front windows' curtains, she realizes it: there isn't time. She leaves the Father's empty body in the grass and runs up the porch steps. Back into the burning house. I scream through the smoking floor, making every plank my rigid spine, and Lila holds the Daughter as though they'll dance.

———

Falling again, though I don't feel it yet. Legs kicking over the abyss. The terrible gift of flight. Gift nonetheless. Behind me, Dad shouts. He didn't do that last time.

The top of the arc. Bloody hair sticking to my scalp, the nape of my neck. I claw empty air, hold my breath. And my once-body emerges from the shadows. Long violet veins thrumming, weeping through sour cherry flesh.

My left hand finds my right, wraps tight together over the knife's hilt. The only tension in me those two muscular threads up my arms. All else floating free, stomach up my throat, bones rattling loose, brain threatening panicked meltdown escape. I'll miss—I'll lose the knife—I'll fall forever—

But Lila, everything is obvious on the way down, and every other part of me screams: *I will make it back to you.*

Closer, really plummeting now, shot bird, clenching the knife closer, clenching my legs up against me, clenching my teeth shut and my eyes open as my meat becomes everything I see. No clean cuts here, just wounds on wounds, half-formed scabs and huge pearls of yellow fat tucked in the shreds. Blood running over it all in hot rivers. Zombie pulse rumbling through my aching head, shaking everything into pounding oblivion. If Dad's yelling after me, I don't hear it. If he's jumped too, I'll never know.

My body. First friend, never meant to be a prison. Everything that was taken.

The knife. Touches.

Cuts.

I slam into myself, face to flesh, gasping and gagging as the blade drags and my hands slip and I jam my shoes into meat and I do not fall. I plunge forward, headfirst, bloody air vanishing into just blood that coats my nose, tongue, throat—choking, ruining, fucking gross, but what's a little autocannibalism among me? I try to laugh, to crawl forward on my elbows, to follow the new wounds and escape. Membranes split, sinews pop, muscle saws away. I don't get out.

Red darkness, a juicy garnet, a wasp in a figgy grave: the muscular wound crushing my arms to my sides, throttling me in a hot embrace. I'm wriggling into night, sparks of no-air twinkling starlight behind my gore-fused eyelashes. I'll die entombed. Ectopic.

Hands lashing out, dragging me forward, limbs thrashing like this is the deep end. Blade through mausoleum flesh, teeth sticky, stomach full. Through my eyelids, the briefest light. Faintest glow. I dig, scratch, slice jiggling fat, strain against skin—

And I burst through.

Gulping air, still blind but scrubbing caked gore from my eyes. More blood running free around the body's waist, soaking into the pale fabric that shrouds me, escaping from the injury just as I'm escaping. Smoke mingles with blood. Dogs howling into heart beating into doors slamming into you, screaming. My overlarge body trembles, drops—I hold on—and your hands fumble with the clothes tented over my head. *I'm here*, I try to call to you, *I'm safe*, but I just cough up blood. You yank the fabric. Buttons ping off the floor. In other circumstances, this would be a great time.

I blink up at you. Huge, gorgeous woman. Your mouth hanging open. Your shining hair, loosed from its scrunchie, curls free over your shoulders. Firelight flickers on your round face. And your eyes—wide and red and sparkly from tears, I'm so sorry—your big brown eyes stare at me, the sexiest teratoma you know.

"Hey," I croak.

You gasp. Hiccup. Hold out a shaking hand. I crawl into your palm—leaving a bloody mess, I'm so sorry again—and you lift me to eye level. A deep black ring surrounds your irises. You breathe out, "Hey," like you think I might turn to a dandelion seed.

I embrace your thumb, and I'm small in a way that feels safe.

BIRD

BIRDIE, *last of my Daughters, has never understood, and she never will. This is good.*

————

You get me caught up. House on fire, out of control, weirder shit than usual going down. Bad dogs at the door. Worse mother waiting outside. I hold parts of your hand in my tiny palms—your heartbeat jumping hot under my knees—and I keep my eyes on you. Your forehead beads with sweat, and smoke squeezes tears out of your eyes. I look at you like you're an angel, and you look at me like I'm a miracle that surprises even you.

"Are you sure you're not hurt?" I crane my neck to see all of you. Some of your hair might be singed. My eyes sting.

You laugh, and the giggles shake through your wrist. Your palm curls around me, guarding me from the drop. "Birdie, you're covered in blood."

"It's not—" I stop. "Well, it is mine, but not really?"

The floor beneath us groans high and ragged from the fire's heat. Rising above it, my mother calls: "Let me in." A hand slams against the door—the deadbolt rattles, struggling—and you hold me close to your chest.

"Run," I tell you. My mother curses, and the dogs whine. "Upstairs. Now."

"But your body—"

The floor sags in a wild flourish of sparks. Through the hiss and crackle, and with a deafening *thunk*, the deadbolt slides free.

"Don't need it! Run!"

You sprint for the stairs. The door flies open as the dogs rocket in, long white teeth under black smoke. I hold tight to your fingers as you round the first few steps, the tower whirling around us, the floor giving out beneath the dogs' paws just as they jump—

They scrabble onto the ringing, wrought-iron staircase and bounce back to their feet. Drool hangs in loops from their open jaws, sizzling as it drops into the basement, a wound of embers and flames.

In the doorway, amber-glow smoke haloes my mother. Loose strands of silver hair float over her thin cheeks. Her blue eyes fix on the body I've left behind, its limbs sliding across the tilting planks towards the fiery collapse. She reaches for it with scalded hands.

She doesn't see me.

She doesn't look at you either as you ascend in a tight spiral, holding me close to your chest. Your breaths, smoke-scarred and panicked, synchronize with the awful rocking of the staircase over the open, burning hell of the basement. Distant bolts screech, ripping free from 150-year-old moorings, mingling with the baying dogs into a chaotic siren. The stairs pitch, and we scream.

Connie seizes Birdie's body, not knowing her daughter is no longer there, not seeing the blood's meaning beyond the injury, not hearing her husband's raging howls as he paces the miniature abyss that now traps him. The empty basement that he created with my help.

After Connie pulls Birdie's almost-empty dollhouse body down the hall and through the front door's gate of flames, I relinquish the remaining floorboards in a surge of sparks. Connie lays its rooms to rest beside the Father's stiffening body on the lawn. She brushes hair from unseeing eyes, squeezes bloodless fingers. A family, together again.

———

We hold tight to each other as you cry out, tip forward, and land hard, the staircase shuddering around us, barely holding on.

The dogs' howling pursuit turns to awful, calculated silence.

I scramble up your shirt, the cotton gritty with soot beneath my palms, and make it to your shoulder in time to hear you scream. Oh God, Lila—

"Get *away!*" Your legs thrash out, and the dogs snap at your sneakers before ducking to the side, their lips high over their teeth in deadly grins. They weave back and forth in the tight space, a cool and patient waltz. The dogs don't have to kill you. They just have to keep you here until the stairs plummet into the inferno. You twist to avoid another bite, squeaking in terror. For a moment, I hang on your collar over the edge—hot air whooshing up, shooting sparks like meteors—and I gaze down into the basement's blazing hellmouth.

Yeah, the dogs don't have to kill you, but on the other hand, I'm pretty sure they're not *allowed* to kill me. I squeeze my burning eyes shut for a moment and wave my free arm over my head. I jangle myself around like a set of car keys. I screech at them.

You see me. You gasp. "Birdie, *no—*"

The border collie snatches your jean leg in its fangs, and you shriek. The golden retriever lunges forward, stumbles as your free sneaker slams against his jaw.

"Hey!" I wrestle a fingernail-sized shoe off my foot, fling it at the dogs. The fancy patent leather bounces off the retriever's skull, but the border collie's eyes roll in their sockets, find me, and go glassy and still with realization. Its slobbery grip on your jeans loosens. That's all you need.

You yank the cloth free, slam both heels into the border collie's black-and-white-furred ribs, and pancake it against the retriever. Without a sound, they tumble together down the ringing iron stairs in a whirl of silky gold and cropped black-and-white, their legs stiffening, their spines straightening, lost in the spark-dense smoke until—when they hit the fire—it seems they haven't been dogs for a long time. Just reproductions, just toys. Plastic puppies.

I tell myself this. I'll tell it to you as well, whenever you need to hear it.

I can't see my mother anymore. Heat-shimmering dollhouse outlines—the *Matrix* diorama, the violin, the stack of books, the wine bottle—barely cut through the choking cinders. I stumble across your shoulder, up your neck, brush tears from your cheeks. They soak my bloody sleeves anew with saltwater. "Lila?"

In answer, you cup me beneath your chin and scramble up the stairs. Banging your shoulders against the railing, sucking air through your teeth as the scalding metal touches your skin. I press myself against your sweat-damp neck. I do not close my eyes, even when the whining bolts deepen into beam-rending groans, even when hot plaster chunks rain down on us. Even when the staircase's metal fingertips slip from their moorings. We swing in an abrupt, awful arc. Just the railing holds us up now, two lily stalks of wrought iron wilting in the heat.

Your enraged scream is louder than the flames, louder than the wrenching metal, vibrating up and out of your throat like bats from a chimney. You throw yourself forward, clawing at the steep steps one-handed, until at last we flop together on the landing. You pant for a few moments on the soot-stained wool rug. I pull yarn-thick locks of hair away from your ash-covered lips. The fire is coming, but we both know this.

When you sit up, I slide down your shirt into your front pocket. Together, we make eye contact with a sailor-suited mouse child and a Keanu Reeves doll on a narrow windowsill. They nod at us, leap out, and take flight, vanishing into the normal summer sunset.

You get to your feet, shoulders heaving. "We're never coming back here."

"There won't be a here to come back to," I say.

Behind us, the staircase lets go, and the empty tower swirls with an inferno of glittering sparks.

––––––––––

Pinned into the struts and bolts of the staircase, I hold steady even as I lighten and lose form. Birdie and Lila fight their way up the stairs, and floor separates from beam. The not-dogs tumble into oblivion, and wallpaper curls from plaster. I part from what I thought was myself, and I find that I am still whole.

The Father and Connie and the not-dogs and me, loyal in all the wrong ways. I've taken an eternity just to realize this: my gaze was never meant to stop at what I could see from the windows. Now, the dolls fill the sky, looking farther than I ever have.

————

"Down the hall," I tell you, coughing. We go together through the smoke. You speed walk the way you're supposed to in an emergency. The fire's roar and crackle dims, though smoke still crowds the ceiling like storm clouds over the empty dollhouses. Little manacles of clear glue are the only trace of their former tenants. "Third door on the left."

You pinch your shirt above your nose to filter the air. Your shea butter soap and rose detergent smell rises. I inhale too deeply and start hacking up a lung again. With one finger—and all the tenderness in the world—you rub my back.

As we reach it, my bedroom door swings open. You stride into the room, catch sight of the ash-smeared suburbia on the walls, and wrinkle your nose.

"Whoa." You stand on your tiptoes to see into the abandoned houses beyond the white picket fences, then touch the quilt on the twin mattress tucked beneath the looming dioramas like a tomb. "Birdie, is this—?"

A pang goes through me at the sight of your hand on the quilt. I want to bundle up the fabric, fling it out the window, try to find some trace of home-smell under the soot. "Yeah." I clear my throat. "Welcome to my room."

"Wow. Um. You outgrew it."

"Probably the last time I'll outgrow anything," I say as you move to the open window. "Never thought I'd be showing it to another girlfriend. Never thought it'd be safe to—but I guess it still isn't, huh?"

You offer me your hand to climb onto, lift me in front of your face. Your warm brown gaze, bloodshot from smoke, flicks between my eyes.

A cool breeze floods into my childhood bedroom, smelling like all the summer evenings when I snuck out. Grass, dew, the endless earth under stars. It's like the house itself is inhaling. We know that we have just enough time.

"Thank you for coming to get me." I have trouble looking at you. It's like looking at God when you know you've done something wrong. Like I can taste honey-tart apples on my tongue, but I want to tell God that I adore Her. "I should've listened to you. I'm sorry."

"Listening to me would've been good," you say, your voice strained with the effort of keeping things light. "But—babe. Hey. Thanks for letting me be the bigger person."

You giggle as my mouth drops open. "*Wow.*"

I laugh after I say it, but you watch me without speaking, and my smile slides away. I let it go.

"I don't think I've grown at all," I tell you, touching one hand to the dimple in your chin. "I think I might be small like this forever."

"Maybe," you agree. And you kiss me, your lips brushing from my jaw to my collarbone. Soft heat blooms to the very tips of my bloody ears.

"I love you, Bird," you say into my heart, and I lean down, press my mouth to the groove of your Cupid's bow.

"I love you too."

We kiss in my childhood bedroom—empty of dolls, alone at last—as the house burns down outside.

———

I breathe in the world beyond the window and hold the lovers in my palms. Elsewhere, banisters become ropes of embers, ceilings great pools of flame, floorboards opalescent coals. House after empty house after empty house falls into itself. Roofs collapse like butterflies closing their wings.

Someday, sunlight will touch the soil here, and then shade. Wildflowers ringed by maples and oak and dark-eyed birch. In the cool shade, moss will grow on the basement stones, so carefully laid by hands long dead. Fungi will sprout in the corners and in the little wildernesses where stones meet. The small creatures in the cellar hole will make their own homes.

And somewhere far above them, spectral feet will rest on open air. Swallows will pass unknowing through gentle hands. Stars will shine on lips touching lips.

Suffering is not the only ghost.

Our voices intertwine as I guide you out the window—*Like this? Almost, just put your hand a bit higher*—and onto the sturdy branches of the walnut tree. Your trembling fingers find the right places and hold tight, and we move together, floating over empty space—*I'm afraid. I know, but you're doing great*—your feet tensing on the swaying bough, my fingertips stroking against your quick-rising chest, and we grip—gasp—descend together, shimmy down through the thick, silky summer leaves and the amber sparks that flit among their undersides, pale and soft as inner wrists. In the dusk, the first fireflies move across the meadow.

Your feet find the ground, your laugh finds your lips, your lips find mine again. You lift me from your pocket to carry me in the free air. You unclip your keys from your belt. We walk to your car, parked next to mine. The house is sun-hot on our backs, sharp splitting cracks echoing from it as you unlock the car—glint of burning beams on the key, funhouse mirror flame on the bug-spattered windows. My mother glances your way before she returns to watching the house's bonfire reaching fire-fingers towards the evening clouds. She's kneeling alongside my body and my father's, long shadows cast behind the three of them. She still doesn't see me.

Your hand opening the door. Your car rumbling to life. Your smile, your soot-covered face, my laugh, my blood-covered body. Us, shaking. You, hitting the gas. Me, my tiny hummingbird heart thrumming as the screaming tires spray gravel in our wake, and the windows of the burning house explode in glittering fireworks, and you hold one warm hand out to me—and we're alive, we're alive, we're alive.

———

The lovers vanish among the leaves. They will never know what I have done for them, my children, and I have never been more joyful. The last dolls scatter from the house, soar among the sparks, outpace the ash until they are only bird-spots against the great summer clouds. I lay my fingertips against warm glass. A carriage is coming through the deep woods. A ship through the lilac sky. A gentle-faced friend through the centuries. I am in the attic, at the window. I am waiting for them.

ACKNOWLEDGMENTS

Thank you to Psychopomp for giving my weird dollhouse novella a home: Sean, Elise, Laura, and Melissa have treated this work with care, curiosity, and encouragement throughout the publication process. Thank you for answering all my questions. The Deadlands was my short fiction debut, and I'm so grateful to have my first book published with you too.

I'm thankful as well to the team behind Apex Snap Judgment 8, who read an earlier draft of the opening and provided useful feedback, and to AJ Super, who mentored me through SFWA's Career Mentorship Program and helped me research markets.

To Nicole, Brendan, Mar, and Ash, thank you so much for your critiques and enthusiastic margin comments. To my parents, thank you for encouraging my writing since childhood. And to Aaron, thank you for loving me and believing in me. Thank you for reading, and rereading, and revising, and reminding me that I don't have to do it alone.

* 9 7 9 8 8 9 1 1 6 0 2 1 7 *